I0681382

THE
GUNSMITH
GIANT

THE JINGLE BELL TRAIL

A Giant Christmas Gunsmith

SPEAKING VOLUMES, LLC
NAPLES, FLORIDA
2020

The Jingle Bell Trail

Copyright © 2020 by Robert J. Randisi

All rights reserved. No part of this book may be reproduced
or transmitted in any form or by any means without written
permission.

This is a work of fiction. Names, characters, places, and
incidents are either the product of the author's imagination or
are used fictitiously, and any resemblance to actual persons,
living or dead, business establishments, events, or locales is
entirely coincidental.

ISBN 978-1-64540-345-6

THE
GUNSMITH
GIANT

THE JINGLE BELL TRAIL

A Giant Christmas Gunsmith

J.R. ROBERTS

Chapter One

Clint Adams didn't usually pay any attention to Christmas. That was probably because he had spent the last twenty or so alone, out on the trail. So it wasn't a holiday he kept track of. That's why he was surprised when he rode into the town of Buckley, North Dakota and found it ostentatiously turned out for the holiday.

Of course, Clint knew it was winter because it was snowing. Thanksgiving had passed with him eating out under the stars, a dinner of bacon-and-beans. Now, riding through North Dakota's snow-covered terrain, wearing a new sheepskin coat he'd bought for himself, he knew only that it was cold and wet, but he didn't mind. He spent so much time in the heat of the Southwest that this was a nice change.

When he saw the sign announcing that Buckley was only six miles away, he decided to stop for a hot meal. Little did he know that he would enter a town that had decked all its halls in a major way.

There was garland everywhere, hanging not only from light posts, but from the second and third floor windows and balconies that lined the main street. There was also plenty of green and red ribbons and, finally, a hand drawn sign stretched over the street that said

MERRY CHRISTMAS. And underneath, in smaller print, ON THE JINGLE BELL TRAIL.

"Toby," he said, to his horse, "I guess it's Christmas."

This was also his first ride without his Darley Arabian, Eclipse. His new four-year-old Tobiano/Red Roan mix, Toby, had performed admirably. He would probably never be as fast and majestic as Duke, his black gelding, and Eclipse had both been, but he was well-formed and unusual looking enough to attract attention.

Tobiano Paints were usually white, with patches of brown or grey, but this one's patches were red. He was also the largest Paint Clint had ever seen.

Toby had snorted his disapproval the first time they encountered snow, because he was used to the Southwest. It took a lot of soothing talk and handling to calm him down and get him to walk on it. But after the first few miles, he seemed to settle down.

Clint reined in the Tobiano in front of The Red Man Saloon. After tying the horse off, he went inside. He was putting off his hot meal and coffee until he could have a cold beer.

The interior of the saloon, mostly empty at the moment, had also been strung with garland, fresh pine and ribbon.

"Merry Christmas," the middle-aged bartender greet-ed him. "What can I getcha?"

"I've lost track of time. When is Christmas?"

"Two weeks," the man said, with a smile. "You've still got time to shop."

"I'm afraid I have nobody to shop for," Clint said. "How about a beer?"

"You look cold."

"I'm going to have a hot meal after this," Clint said, "but first I need a beer."

"Comin' up."

"Looks like this town goes all out for Christmas," Clint said, as the man drew his beer.

"Oh, that we do." He set the cold beer mug down in front of Clint.

"I saw the sign over the street," Clint said. "What's the Jingle Bell Trail? I've never heard of it."

"Ah," the bartender said, "that's local. It's a road leading from here to the town of Goodwill."

"Goodwill?"

The bartender's smile broadened, and his cheeks red-dened.

"You think we decorate for Christmas, you should see them," he said. "Since both towns turn out for Christmas every year, we decided to name the road between us the Jingle Bell Trail."

"I guess that makes sense. But this town is called Buckley. What's that got to do with Christmas?"

"Nothin'," the barman said. "We're takin' steps to change the name, though."

"To what?" Clint sipped his frigid beer. Even though he was cold, it felt good going down his throat.

"That's the problem," he said. "The mayor and the town council can't agree on one."

"I guess there are so many possibilities," Clint commented.

The bartender leaned on the bar.

"My suggestion is Silent Night."

"Like the Christmas carol?"

"Why not? That song dates back to eighteen-eighteen. It's recognizable right away."

"I suppose it is," Clint said. "What are the other suggestions?"

"I don't get to know that," the barman said. "I ain't on the council."

"Ah."

Abruptly, the man stood up straight and stuck his hand out. Clint took it. For a rather pudgy fellow, he had a hearty handshake.

"The name's Chris."

"Clint."

"You look like you been ridin' a while, and it's only gonna get colder," Chris said. "The Holly House is our best hotel, just up the street."

"Holly House?" Clint repeated.

"Yep," Chris said. "We celebrate Christmas all year 'round. Anyway, they got good beds and a fine restaurant if you like steaks."

"I love steaks," Clint said.

"Well, there ya go, then," Chris said. "No reason not to stay the night."

"No, I guess not." Clint finished his beer. "Down the street, you said?"

"Coupla blocks," Chris said. "And there's a livery stable right behind it."

"You're making it hard to resist," Clint said. "Thanks, Chris. What do I owe you?"

"First one's on the house," Chris said. "Sort of a Christmas present. Come on back after you eat. It'll be more lively here, tonight."

"I'll do that," Clint said, "thanks, again."

He turned and left.

Chapter Two

Clint entered the Holly Hotel and found the lobby decked out in fresh evergreen garland, holly, and ribbons. In one corner was a huge pine tree covered in glass ornaments and candles that would be lighted after dark. On another side, a fireplace had a roaring fire surrounded by paper decorations. Clint hoped the hotel staff knew what they were doing.

He approached the front desk and said to the smiling clerk, "This is very impressive."

"Thank you, sir," the clerk said. "We want all of our visitors and guests to feel the Christmas spirit as soon as they enter."

The lobby looked to Clint like the inside of a child's dream. He was impressed by the amount of work that had gone into it, and so "impressive" was the word he came up with.

"Can we help you, sir?"

"I just rode into town. The bartender at the Red Man Saloon told me you had the best rooms and beds in town."

"That would've been Chris," the well-dressed, well-groomed young clerk said. "Yes, sir, we pride ourselves on seeing to our guest's comforts."

"He also told me you had good steaks in your dining room," Clint went on.

"We have the finest cook in town in our kitchen," the clerk bragged.

"Well then, I guess I better see if I can get a room before you fill up."

"A wise decision, sir," the clerk said. "Please sign our register and I'll be happy to give you a room."

He turned the register book around and handed Clint a quill pen. Clint scrawled his name. Where it asked him to write where he was from, he wrote Las Vegas, New Mexico, which had replaced Labyrinth, Texas as his preferred stopover between rides, these days. It was also where he had left Eclipse in the care of his friend, John Locke, who had a ranch there.

"Mr. . . . Adams!" the clerk blurted, as he read the name. "Ah, yes sir, let me give you a different room." The clerk replaced the first key he had taken off a hook and grabbed another one. "It's larger and much more comfortable, sir."

"Thank you."

"Is there anything else I can do? Carry your bags? Care for your horse?"

"I'm told you have a livery out back," Clint said.

"Yes, we do, sir," the clerk said. "Otto is our hostler. He knows his business. I can have him come around and—"

"That's okay," Clint said. "I'll walk my horse around back myself."

"Yes, sir, of course," the clerk said, nervously. "Anything you want."

Clint went outside, untied the Tobiano and walked the animal around to the back. As he approached the door, a large man stepped out to meet him. Clint wondered if the clerk had run back and told the man to expect him. And who he was.

"Are you Otto?" he asked.

"That's me," the large man said. "That's a fine looking young animal."

"Yes, it is."

"I always heard the Gunsmith rode a big black."

"We all get put out to pasture sooner or later," Clint said. "This is Toby."

"Toby the Tobiano?" Otto said, raising his eyebrows. "That ain't very original."

"It wasn't my idea, and by the time I got him, he was answering to it."

Otto reached out, and Clint handed him the reins.

"I'll unsaddle him and see to him," the big man said.

"Be careful he doesn't drink too much water—"

"I've been takin' care of horses for forty years, Mr. Adams," Otto said. "I know what to do."

"Of course," Clint said. "Sorry. Oh, I'll take my saddlebags."

He removed them, and Otto walked Toby into the livery. Clint turned and went back to the hotel.

Chapter Three

Both the bartender and the clerk were right about the steaks in the dining room. The one Clint had was perfectly cooked and accompanied by vegetables, including carrots like Clint had never had before. They virtually melted in his mouth.

"Can I get you anythin' else, Mr. Adams?" the waiter asked. Clint hadn't told him his name.

"Yes," Clint said, "do you have any pie?"

"Yes, our cook does a wonderful apple-and-cinnamon pie for the Christmas season."

"I'll have a slice of that and a cup of coffee," Clint said.

"Comin' right up."

Clint didn't know what apple and cinnamon had to do with Christmas, but after his first bite, he thought that it should be a regular Christmas treat around the world.

When he finished, he paid his bill and went to his room, which was clean and well furnished. So far, Buckley was a model town, right down to reading material Clint found on the night table. It was a hardcover copy of Charles Dickens' *A Christmas Carol*. He wondered if there was a copy in every room?

He had a Mark Twain in his saddlebags but decided instead to start reading the Dickens. He had read *Oliver Twist* and enjoyed it very much, so this would be his second of the British author's works. And, considering where he was and the time of the year, it was appropriate.

He read up to the point where the Ghost of Christmas past was going to appear, then set the book aside and went to sleep in the warm, comfortable bed.

***

He woke the next morning feeling refreshed from having slept in a real bed. It took a while for him to crawl out from beneath the warm covers, wash and get dressed. He felt chilled already as he went down the stairs, but when he reached the lobby, it was warm from the fireplace.

He went into the dining room for a breakfast of bacon-and-eggs, washed down by a pot of hot, strong coffee. He was finishing up when a man wearing a badge appeared in the doorway from the lobby. He was tall, in his forties, wearing a sheepskin lined jacket with a scarf tucked into the neck. The holstered pistol on his left hip had a worn grip, as if it had been well-used. He looked around the half-filled dining room, spotted Clint and came walking over. Clint had been afraid the man was looking for him.

"Mr. Adams?" he said, in a deep bass voice.

"That's right."

"I heard you were in town," he went on. "I hope I'm not interruptin' your breakfast."

"I just finished, Sheriff," Clint said. "Care to help me drain this coffee pot?"

"A hot cup of coffee sounds good."

"Have a seat, then."

The man sat, removed the gloves he was wearing and set them down on the table. Clint poured him a cup of coffee, then refilled his own cup. He signaled the waiter for another pot.

"That's good," the lawman said, taking a sip.

"More coming," Clint said. "What can I do for you, Sheriff?"

"My name's Matt Owens, Mr. Adams," the sheriff said. "I realize we don't know each other, so I'm goin' way out on a limb here."

"Part of the job, isn't it?" Clint asked. "Going out on a limb?"

"You're right about that," the lawman agreed. He drank some more coffee. His cheeks were red and raw, as if he had been out on the trail all night.

"Here's some more," Clint said, as the waiter appeared and refilled both their cups.

"Anythin' else, sir?" he asked Clint.

"We're fine," Clint said. "Just leave the pot and take the empty."

"Yessir."

The waiter did as he was told and withdrew.

"Are you the local law, Sheriff?"

"I'm the county sheriff," Owens said. "My office is in Goodwill, but I get to this end of the Jingle Bell trail pretty often."

"What brings you here today?"

"I'm trackin' three men," Sheriff Owens said. "They burned out a ranch near here, killed the rancher and his wife."

"Why'd they do that?"

"I'll ask 'em when I catch 'em," Owens said. "I had to hit the trail after them without a posse or let them put too many miles between us."

"I can understand that."

"And I don't have a deputy I could've taken with me," Owens went on. "When I got to Buckley, I heard talk that the Gunsmith was in town."

"That happens," Clint admitted. "When I arrive in town, word tends to get around."

"I'm gonna ask you for somethin' I've got no right to ask," Owens said.

"What's that?"

"A favor."

Chapter Four

"I'm listening," Clint said.

"That alone is probably more than I have a right to expect," Owens said. "The three men I'm tracking are bad ones. I'm not sure I'm gonna be able to bring them in alone."

"You look like a man who knows his job," Clint said. "That gun on your hip has seen its day."

"It has," Owens said, "and so have I. But I've got a wife and a small boy at home, and I'd like to get back to them before Christmas. Actually, I'd like to get back to them, period, but by Christmas would be good, too. My boy says he wants to be a lawman, and I'm gonna pin a badge on him as a present."

"How old is he?"

"Five."

"He'll be thrilled."

"If I get home to do it."

"So let me get this straight," Clint said. "You pretty much want me to help you get home for Christmas."

"That's it."

"Why don't you forget about those three and just go home to your family?"

"Because I've got a job to do," Owens said. "As much as I wanna see my boy, I've gotta do my job. I'm a lawman, have been for more than twenty years. But I know my limitations. I'm not about to face three men with guns."

"And what will you do if I say no?" Clint asked.

"I'd have to track 'em and pick them off one-by-one."

"Ambush?"

"Not necessarily," Owens said. "If I can separate them, I can take them one-on-one. But if not . . ." He shrugged.

"I don't like the idea of bushwhacking anyone," Clint said. "Not even an outlaw."

"They're not just outlaws, Mr. Adams," Owens said, "they're killers."

"You know this for sure?"

"Oh yeah," Owens said. "The rancher talked before he died, named the three men. One of them actually worked for him for a while. Apparently he got the job just to case the place."

"Big ranch?"

"One of the biggest in the county," Owens said. "I'm under pressure to bring these three back, dead or alive."

"Political pressure?"

"That, too," Owens said, "but I want to do it to show the people I'm on the job."

"I don't like rich ranchers, or politicians," Clint said.

"Fred Cummings was more than just a rich rancher," Owens said. "He was one of Goodwill's model citizens, did a lot of volunteer work, donated a lot of money. I know the kind of ranchers you're talkin' about, and Fred wasn't one of them. He was good people, him and his wife." Owens sat back in his chair. "Just talkin' about it makes me want a drink."

Clint waved the waiter over.

"Do you have something to sweeten this coffee with?" he asked.

"Sugar, sir?"

"No," Clint said, "something liquid."

"Yessir, right away."

The waiter went to the kitchen, came back with a pitcher. He poured a generous dollop of brown liquid into their coffee cups.

"Pour the rest of it into the pot," Clint said.

"Yes, sir."

The waiter obeyed and withdrew. Clint could smell the whiskey as he lifted the cup to his lips. It warmed him going down. The sheriff took a generous swallow and sighed.

"Who are the three men?" Clint asked.

"Two of them are Ames and Holloway," the lawman said. "I don't know they're first names. But the one who worked for Cummings was Zack Nelson."

"I don't know that name."

"If he does this for a living, he's been keepin' a low profile," Owens said. "I don't know the name, either."

"Did Cummings catch him in the act?" Clint asked. "Is that why he killed them?"

"He could've left them alive, but it looks like he wanted to kill 'em."

"A man like that will do it again if he's not stopped."

"That's what I think," Owens said, sitting forward in his chair. "Mr. Adams, I'm askin' you this for two reasons. One's obvious. You're the Gunsmith. With you on my side, I'm sure to get home for Christmas."

"And the second reason?"

"I've heard things about you beyond your obvious reputation."

"Is that right?" Clint asked. "And what've you heard, Sheriff?"

Before answering, the sheriff poured them both another cup of the whiskey-soaked coffee. He picked up his cup and raised it to Clint.

"I've heard you're a man who does the right thing," he said.

Chapter Five

"And you think that's fair?" Clint asked. "First invoking Christmas, and then using some lame compliment?"

The sheriff sat back heavily in his chair.

"I'm usin' what I've got, Mr. Adams," he confessed. "I just thought I'd ask."

"What's your plan, Sheriff?" Clint asked.

"I've tracked them this far," the man said. "I mean to pick up the trail again outside of town."

"They didn't ride into town?" Clint asked.

"It doesn't look like it."

"Do you know how much money they got?"

"Not for sure," Owens said. "It's whatever was in Mr. Cummings' safe. Could've been thousands."

"Well, working there, this Zack Nelson would've had some idea how much was there."

"And that's why he hit when he did," Owens said.

"Sheriff," Clint said, "I'm not a man given to enjoying the Christmas spirit, but I admit this town has had its effect on me."

"You'll help me?"

"I'll do it," Clint said, "for your boy. What's his name?"

"Joseph," Owens said. "We call him Joey."

"Let's go and saddle up," Clint said, "and get this done for Joey."

***

Sheriff Owens' horse, a good-looking buckskin, was already saddled and waiting out front. He took the reins and followed Clint around behind the hotel to the livery.

"Are you leavin'?" Otto asked.

"Not for good," Clint said. "I'm just going to ride out and give the sheriff, here, a hand."

"Well, your boy is ready to go. He's rested and fed. Want me to saddle 'im?"

"I can do it myself, Otto, thanks," Clint said.

"Suit yerself."

Clint went in while Owens waited outside. He saddled the Tobiano and walked him out.

"That's quite a horse," Owens said, when he saw Toby. "A Tobiano?"

"He's actually half Red Roan," Clint said.

"That explains the odd red pigment," Owens said.

They mounted up and rode around to the front of the hotel.

If we ride just east of town, we can pick up their trail," Owens said. "Luckily, it hasn't snowed again since I got here. We should be able to see their tracks easily."

"Suits me," Clint said. "Are you a good tracker?"

"I'm not an expert tracker, but like I said, the snow's gonna help."

"Lead the way, then," Clint said.

He followed the sheriff out of town, snow crunching beneath the hooves of their horses.

***

"There," Owens said, about half-an-hour later.

"I see," Clint said, looking down through the mist of his own breath at the tracks left by three horses. "We should be able to find where they camped overnight."

"Hopefully," Owens said, "they didn't split the money and go their separate ways. If they did, I'm gonna be out here a lot longer."

"Let's deal with that if we come to it," Clint suggested.

"Right."

***

Around midday they came to a cold camp.

"Looks like them," Owens said, dismounting and dropping to one knee. "Yeah, one of these horses has the same chip in the left forefront."

"We have a problem over here," Clint said, from the other side of the campsite.

"What is it?" Owens asked, walking over.

"Their horses were picketed here," Clint said. "As you can see, when they saddled up and broke camp, they separated."

"That's just great," Owens said. "I don't know which horse is Zack Nelson's."

Clint continued to walk a bit further from camp, then stopped.

"Change of plans," he called out.

"What plans?" Owens asked. "We don't have any plans."

"Not us," Clint said, "them. Two stayed together, while the third went his own way."

"Well, that's good," Owens said. "That means we don't have three trails to choose from."

"Your horse with the chipped shoe and one other went that way," Clint said, pointing, "and the third man went that way."

"We'll have to split up."

Clint pulled his collar up as a chill ran down his neck. He could just as easily have told the sheriff no, and he'd be back in town with a hot cup of coffee.

"Which trail do you want?" Clint asked.

Chapter Six

The sheriff chose the trail of the two men together.

"I don't think Nelson would ride off alone, and I want him," he said.

"Are you sure?" Clint said. "You asked for my help so you wouldn't have to face more than one man alone."

"I can handle two," Owens assured him.

"Suit yourself," Clint said. "Once we catch up and take them, we can meet back here."

"Agreed," Owens said.

"Good luck to you, Sheriff," Clint said.

They mounted up and each took to their own trail . . .

***

It didn't take long for Clint to catch up to his man. Apparently, his horse had gone lame, and Clint could see by the trail that he eventually dismounted and started walking the animal.

He came to the top of a hill and could see the man just ahead of him, walking slowly, his shoulders hunched against the cold.

Clint had several options. He could circle up ahead of the man, or just keep on the way he was going. There was nothing to indicate he was helping the lawman with his hunt. This man could simply think he was crossing paths with another traveler.

He decided to take his time and just keep riding. Eventually, the man became aware of him, stopped and turned.

As Clint approached, the man waved and put a smile on his face.

"Sure glad you came along," he called out. "My horse's gone lame."

"That's a bad situation, being so cold and all," Clint said.

"Yer tellin' me," the man said. "Afraid I'm gonna need your horse, Mister."

The man went for his gun, but did it nonchalantly, as if he expected no resistance from Clint.

"You pull that hogleg, I'm going to have to kill you where you stand, Mister," he said.

The man froze and asked, "You think you can do that?"

"I know I can. How sure are you that you can draw before I do?"

The man studied him, then moved his hand from his gun.

"You're too damn sure to suit me," he grumbled. "I s'pose you're gonna leave me out here to freeze?"

"No," Clint said, "I'm going to take you back to Buckley and turn you over to the sheriff, who'll take you to Goodwill to stand trial for murder."

The man scowled. That and the dark stubble on his face made him look like he was in his fifties.

"You a deputy?"

"Nope," Clint said, "just doing a favor for the sheriff. He wants to get home to see his boy for Christmas."

"Well, that ain't gonna happen," the man said.

"Oh? Why not?"

"Nelson's waitin' for the lawman to catch up to him," the man said. "Says he's gonna kill 'im."

"So he's expecting him."

"Oh yeah."

"How does he plan on killing him?"

"Nelson's pretty good with a gun," the man said, "but he's got a fella with him named Ames. He makes his livin' with a gun. Nelson figures between them, the lawman ain't got a chance."

That was bad. There was no way Clint could catch up to the sheriff to warn him, not with this man and his lame horse in tow.

"Mister, I think you may have just lucked out," Clint told the man.

"How's that?"

"I *am* going to leave you here, like you said. You're on your own."

"On this lame horse?" the man complained. "I'll freeze to death."

"You should've thought of that before you robbed that ranch and killed a man and his wife."

"I robbed him, all right, but it was Nelson who done the killin'. Look, I'll give ya my share, just don't leave me here. It's goddamned cold!"

"I don't need your share," Clint said. "You'll get what you deserve, out here."

Clint started to turn the Tobiano, but the man decided to make a play.

"You sonofa—" he said, grabbing his gun.

Clint drew and fired. Before the man even realized what had happened, he was dead.

"I guess you'll keep," Clint said.

Too bad he had to leave the horse out there, but he had to try and catch up to the sheriff.

***

Clint pushed the Tobiano harder than he ever had before. He knew the general direction the sheriff had gone, but instead of going back to the point where they split up, he took a diagonal tact, hoping to intercept the man before he walked into a trap.

He hadn't wanted to kill the third man, but it turned out to be the best thing. He didn't have to worry about letting him go, now. And once he joined the sheriff and they took care of Nelson and Ames, they could come back and collect the body and his share of the money.

Clint finally reached a point where he could see the horse's tracks in the snow. He recognized the hoof print with the chipped horseshoe and saw the third set of tracks left by Sheriff Owens, who was trailing them.

And then it started to snow.

Toby didn't like the flurries hitting him in the face, and neither did Clint. Luckily, he had already spotted the tracks, so he was pretty sure he was going in the right direction as the new fallen snow started to cover them.

Before long the tracks were completely covered, and he couldn't see very far ahead of him. Hopefully, the others were having the same problem. If Sheriff Owens couldn't find the two killers, then Clint had time to catch him.

When Clint did catch up, it was a shock. He could barely see a foot in front of him, but when he saw the sheriff, he was right there in front of him.

"Jesus," he said, reining in.

He dismounted and walked over to the man who was lashed to a tree. There was no telling how long he had been dead. His gun was gone from his holster and there were two bullet holes in his chest. The blood that had flowed from them was now frozen.

"Sonofabitch!" he swore, as he realized two things. One, he was going to have to track Nelson and Holloway and make them pay, and two, he was going to have to tell Sheriff Owens' wife, and his son Joey, that he was dead.

Chapter Seven

Clint cut the man down, but he wasn't able to bury him, not in that driving snow, with the ground so hard and cold. He wrapped Owens' body with his blanket, tied it tight in case any critter tried to get to it, and set it down at the base of the tree. He would pick him up on the way back.

He couldn't camp, not when the driving snow made it impossible to build a fire. Also, he had no blanket since he had wrapped the lawman's body in it. So all he could do was mount the Tobiano and continue on. Maybe he'd come to some sort of cover where he could sit the blizzard out. Then he would have to decide if he should take Owens' body back to Buckley, or even Goodwill, or continue on after the two killers.

He was also hoping that, somewhere along the way, he would come across the sheriff's horse. If he was going to have to tie Owens' body to the Tobiano, it would take them forever to get back to Buckley. For that reason alone, he might have to leave the body where it was and continue on.

He could feel the Tobiano's discomfort beneath him. The young horse was probably close to refusing to go any further, especially not into the teeth of the storm. But at that moment he could also feel a difference in the wind. Almost abruptly the snow stopped, and the wind died down.

Clint reined the Tobiano in and dismounted, stood in front of the horse, stroked him and spoke in soothing tones.

"I know you want to go back, but we have to keep on going," Clint said. "I agreed to help the sheriff, and I can't stop now."

With the driving snow stopped, he took a look around, hoping to see something in the distance. But there was only white. Suddenly, he missed the Southwest very, very much—especially the heat.

He mounted up and started riding. There were no more tracks to follow, so all he could do was continue to ride in the same direction.

***

He saw the smoke first. When he reached it, he saw that it was a barn, burning. Across from the barn was a house that had not caught fire . . . yet. There was also a well, with two horses tied to it.

He dismounted and left the Tobiano tied to a tree. Making his way on foot to the well, he kept a sharp eye out on the house in case someone came out.

When he reached the well, he lifted the left forefront of each horse, found the one with the chip. That meant he had caught up to the killers, and they were inside. Hopefully, they hadn't killed this rancher, yet.

Clint moved from the well to the barn, which was still burning. The heat from the fire felt good, but he was more concerned with whether or not there was anyone inside. He looked through the front doors, didn't see any bodies on the floor of the barn, or any horses in the stalls. There was a corral next to it, which was empty.

He left the heat of the fire, and by the time he reached the small house, he was chilled once again. He glanced in a window, saw two men with guns standing over a man and a woman seated at a small kitchen table. It was the rancher and his wife, obviously. They hadn't killed them yet, for some reason, but he didn't know how long they had, so he was going to have to do something.

He could have just shot them through the window, but that was the same as back shooting a man, and he couldn't countenance that. When he shot a man, it had to be from the front, face-to-face.

He walked around to the front of the house, stepped to the door and kicked it open.

Chapter Eight

"What the hell—" one of the men said, as they both turned.

"Which one of you is Nelson?" Clint asked.

"I am," the older man said.

Clint looked at the other man, who was about ten years younger.

"That makes you Holloway."

"Help us!" the woman cried.

"Shut up!" Nelson snapped. He looked at Clint. Both he and Holloway had their hands down at their sides, near their guns. "What do you want?"

"I want the two of you, for murder in Goodwill, and for killing Sheriff Owens."

"What are you, his deputy?" Nelson asked.

"No," Clint said, "I'm just doing him a favor."

"By gettin' killed?" Nelson asked, grinning.

"By bringing you back," Clint said, "dead or alive. I've already taken care of your other man."

"Holloway," Nelson said. "His horse went lame, so we left him. I figured the law would catch up to him."

"I did," Clint said, "and the sheriff caught up to the two of you and you killed him."

"He deserved to die," Nelson said. "He arrested me once before, but I escaped. I had to get back at him and take care of Cummings at the same time."

"And why these two?" Clint asked. "Why burn their barn and kill them?"

Nelson shrugged.

"Why not? We needed a place to stay, somethin' to eat. I enjoyed killing Cummings and his wife, so why not another husband-and-wife?" He waved at the two middle-aged people seated at the table.

"So why set their barn on fire," Clint said.

Nelson's smile broadened even more.

"We needed the heat."

"All right," Clint said, "now you've got two choices, drop your guns or skin them. Take your pick."

"One of us can kill these two, while the other one kills you," Nelson said.

"Do it, then."

Holloway spoke for the first time.

"Don't, Nelson."

"Why not?"

"This fella," Holloway said, "he knows his way around a gun. Look at the way he stands."

"This is why I got you, Holloway," Nelson said, "To handle men who know their way around guns. You take him, and I'll kill these two."

"Don't—" Holloway started, but it was too late. Nelson went for his gun, and that committed them both.

Even though Nelson drew first, Clint knew he had to take Holloway. The man was surprisingly faster than his boss. Clint drew and shot Holloway in the stomach, then turned his gun on Nelson as the man pointed his weapon at the seated couple. The husband quickly tried to cover his wife's body with his own.

Clint shot Nelson, who dropped his gun to the floor, and then fell face down on it.

Clint moved quickly, checked the two bodies to make sure they were dead, kicking their guns away, in any case. He then ejected his spent shells, replaced them and holstered his gun.

"Omigod!" the woman shrieked. "Thank you, thank you. They were going to kill us."

Clint looked at the stove, where there was a pot bubbling.

"Were they going to make you feed them first?" he asked.

"Y-yes," she said. "I had a pot of stew on the stove when they broke in."

"But you're both all right?" Clint asked.

"We're fine, now," the man said. "Thanks to you." He stood and put his hand out. "My name's Stuart Talmage, this is my wife, Emily."

"Mr. Talmage," Clint said shaking the man's hand. "I'm Clint. Why don't we carry these two bodies outside?"

"I don't want to bury them on my land," Talmage said angrily.

"I don't, either," Clint said, "but I really don't want to have to ride back to Buckley with them tied to their horses. It's too cold, and it'll take me too long. Besides, they killed a lawman and I have to take him back to his family."

"I have an idea," Talmage said.

"What is it?"

"Let me show you."

They took Holloway's body by the shoulders and feet and carried him outside.

"Over there," Talmage said, and Clint knew what he meant.

They tossed the gunman's body into the burning barn, and then did the same with Nelson's.

"Why don't you fetch your horse?" Talmage said. "Bring him in, and I'll put him in the bunkhouse. It's empty. After that you can get warm with some of Emily's stew."

"That sounds good," Clint said, and went to get the Tobiano.

Chapter Nine

When Toby was unsaddled and "bedded down" in the bunkhouse, out of the cold, Clint sat down to a bowl of Emily Talmage's hot stew.

"This is wonderful," he told her, as he chewed. "I really thought I'd freeze to death, out there. Especially when the storm, whipped up."

"That was when they broke in here," Talmage said, "to get out of the storm."

"They were talkin' about how they was gonna kill us after they ate," Emily said. "It was frightenin'."

"We're sure glad you come along when you did," her husband said.

"I'm sort of glad, too," Clint said. "I didn't know how long I was going to have to track them. At least this way I get a hot meal in my belly before I go back out and take Sheriff Owens' body back to his family."

"That's so sad," Emily said. "It's Christmas, after all. Are there children?"

"A five-year-old boy."

A tear rolled down Emily's cheek. "We never had no kids, but . . . that's just so sad."

"You'll spend the night," Stu Talmage said, "give you and your horse some rest."

Clint hated the thought of leaving Owens' body out there, but it made sense to get some rest and an early start in the morning.

"I appreciate that," Clint said.

"And that'll give me one more chance to get a hot meal into your belly," Emily said. "I'll make ya a good breakfast."

"I'm much obliged, Ma'am."

"We're the ones obliged to you, Mister," she said. "You saved our lives."

There was only one bedroom, so Clint bedded down on the floor near the fireplace. True to her word, Emily Talmage gave him a good, hearty and warm breakfast the next morning before he headed out. He left the two outlaws' horses and saddles for the Talmages, which was probably not a fair exchange for their burnt-out barn.

***

Initially, Clint couldn't find Sheriff Owens' body.

He retraced his steps, and even though the weather was clear, with no new storm in sight, the white snow on the ground just made everything look the same. But there was no way he was returning to Buckley without the body.

He tried to come up with some sort of search pattern, and luckily was able to see his own tracks in the snow. He wouldn't end up covering the same ground more than once.

By the time he found the body, Emily Talmage's hot breakfast had cooled considerably in his belly, and he felt the chill. He thought he saw the brown of his blanket several times. Finally he dismounted, walked to a tree that looked familiar and found it. He had to dig it out of the snow, and then was able to hoist it up onto his horse, just behind the saddle, and tie it into place. He mounted up then and gave the Tobiano his head, so he could set his own comfortable pace.

***

Clint rode into Buckley just before dark, which pleased him. He did not want to be caught out in that frigid weather overnight. The town was just starting to light candles they had put out for Christmas, so it was easy to spot from a distance. The Tobiano not only saw the light, but probably smelled civilization and increased his tempo on his own. When Clint reined in the horse in front of the livery stable, the Tobiano took a huge breath and let it out gratefully.

"Whataya got there, a body?" Otto, the hostler asked, coming out.

"Sheriff Owens, from Goodwill," Clint said.

"Aw damn," Otto said. "He was a good man. What happened?"

Clint told the man about tracking the killers and how he had agreed to help the man track them from Buckley.

"Sonsofbitches," Otto said. "I'm glad you got 'em, Mr. Adams."

"I need to get him to Goodwill and his family," Clint said, "so I'm going to need a buckboard and a horse. Can I rent one from you?"

"No, sir," Otto said, "but you can borrow 'em. I can have it rigged up for you in the mornin'."

"That'll work," Clint said, "I just have to keep the body someplace overnight. Can you help me get it to the undertaker?"

"Forget the undertaker," Otto said. "It's cold enough for me to keep it right here til mornin', and it won't stink, or nothin'."

"Much obliged, Otto."

"I'm doin' it for the sheriff," Otto said. "He's got family in Goodwill, don't he?"

"He does," Clint said, "A wife and a little boy."

"Damn, that's gonna make for a tough Christmas."

"It sure is."

"Well," Otto said, "you get yourself some rest, Mr. Adams, and I'll have everythin' ready for you come mornin'."

"I appreciate it, Otto," Clint said, and headed into his hotel.

Chapter Ten

Clint got his clothes changed, tossing the cold, damp shirt and jeans into a corner. But he needed more than a change of clothes to warm up, so he went to the saloon for a whiskey. While it burned its way down to his belly, he crossed over to the dining room and ordered a bowl of soup before having a steaming steak-and-vegetables supper.

After pie and coffee, he went back across the lobby to the saloon for another whiskey, and a beer. The saloon was basically for the hotel guests, so there was no gambling, no music, just a few girls working the floor while guests stood or sat around, enjoying a drink or two. This suited Clint, as he wasn't in the mood for the usual saloon noise. He took his drinks to a table and sat, wondering how he was going to break the news to a five-year-old boy—on Christmas—that his father was dead.

After a while, one of the girls came over and sat across from him.

"You look sad and lonely," she said to him. "Don't you know it's Christmas season?"

"That's part of the problem," he told her. "I've got to deliver some bad news to a family."

"Oh." She looked at his beer mug. "Do you want another drink, honey?"

"Sure," he said, "I'll take another beer."

But he had more than just another . . .

***

When he woke the next morning, Clint realized he could have been dead. He looked at the naked girl next to him, didn't remember bringing her to his room, didn't recall anything after a few more beers. His gun was hanging on the bedpost, so at least he'd had the wherewithal for that, but if anyone had broken into his room during the night, he'd be dead—unless his instincts took over, even while drunk.

The girl was naked, full-bodied, lying on her belly with her big breasts flattened beneath her. He frowned, studied her, realized it was the saloon girl who had come to sit with him. He didn't remember her name, if she had ever given it to him. She had long dark hair that lay over her back like a blanket but didn't reach her chunky buttocks. The flesh of her lovely thighs and legs was as smooth as silk.

She had probably taken his mind off his unpleasant task in more ways than one.

Clint left the bed, went to the dresser and poured himself a glass of water from the pitcher there. He drank it down, turned and looked at the sleeping girl again and felt a stirring that even a hangover could not quell.

He went back to the bed and slipped in next to her. At that moment she moved, turned her head to look at him and smiled.

"You're awake," she said.

"Just," he said. "Um, what happened last night?"

Her smile broadened. She rolled onto her left side, propped her head up with her hand, exposing her breasts and pubic bush to him, completely capturing his attention. It was nice to know that, even blackout drunk, he knew exactly the kind of woman he preferred.

"You don't remember?" she asked. "Not anythin'?"

"Well, not much," he admitted.

She reached out to run her fingernails over him as his body continued to react.

"We gave each other early Christmas presents," she said.

"We did?"

"Oh yes," she said, "you did things to me no other man has ever done."

"I hope it was, uh, what you wanted," he said.

"It was what I wanted," she assured him, "only I never knew I wanted it until you did it."

Clint frowned. Parts of his body were throbbing in a good way, but his head was throbbing in a bad one. Still, he thought he understood her.

"If you like," she said, pushing herself up into a seated position and running both hands through her long hair. "If you want, we can do it all again now that you're relatively sober—you know, just to remind us." The movement raised her breasts so that the nipples pointed at him. She remained that way for a few moments, just to let him have a look.

"That might be a good idea," he said. "I have a feeling that was a night I'm not going to want to forget."

She laughed.

"That's what you said during the night," she told him, "while you were makin' me a very happy girl."

"Then I guess we both need to be reminded of what we did?" he said, "since I have to leave town today."

"You told me you were goin' to Goodwill," she said. "That's not very far. I'm sure you'll be comin' back this way again . . . soon?"

He reached out for her and tugged her closer to him.

"I think that can be arranged."

Chapter Eleven

Clint rolled her onto her back so he could kiss her, first on the mouth, then the neck, then the breasts and nipples—where he lingered. She moaned and cradled his head, used her nails to scratch his bare shoulders. Eventually he continued on, kissing her belly and letting his tongue leave a wet trail down to her pubic patch.

"I know I have a lot of hair there," she said. "I hope it don't bother you."

"I like it," he said, rubbing his face over it. "Are there men who don't?"

"I don't know," she said. "The men I've been with just poke through it and have their way. Nobody's ever done what you did to me last night—what you're doin' now."

"Well," he said, "let me tell you I like doing it, and I like the hair. So you just lie back and enjoy."

He used his tongue to probe through the bush and when he found her moist portal and touched it with the tip of his tongue, she started, as if struck by lightning, and said, "Jesus, don't worry, I'm gonna enjoy!"

***

Later, she rode him hard until her body was wracked by waves of pleasure, and when he exploded inside of her, he roared out loud.

She dropped down on him, lay chest-on-chest for a few minutes, then rolled off him.

"You don't know my name, do you?" she asked.

"Did you tell me your name?"

"Yes."

"Then I forgot it," he admitted. "I'm sorry."

"Don't worry about it," she laughed. "It only matters the way you made me feel."

She got up off the bed, looked around for her dress and pulled it on over her head.

"It's Mitzi," she said. "My name's Mitzi."

He sat up.

"Do I have to pay you?"

"You don't pay for women," she said. "You told me that right away. And now I know why. I should be payin' you."

"Look," he said, "thanks."

"For what?"

"You helped take my mind of my unpleasant task," he said.

"That's right," she said, "you're goin' to Goodwill today."

"Do you know how long a ride that is?" he asked.

She shrugged.

"Coupla hours, I guess."

"You ever been there?"

"Once or twice," she said. "I've gotta go and get some sleep before I go back to work. At my age, I need my rest to compete with the younger girls."

"I can't imagine any of the younger ones can compete with you, Mitzi."

She came to the bed to kiss him goodbye. With her make-up rubbed off, he could see she was in her late thirties. That was old for a saloon girl, which was why she said she needed her sleep.

She walked to the door, then turned to face him again.

"Get your unpleasantness done and then come back this way and see me," she said. "Maybe I'll have somethin' for you for Christmas."

"I'll look forward to that," he said.

She smiled and left.

He laid back down for a moment but got up quickly and quit the bed. He should've already been on the trail with Sheriff Owens' body.

He got up and dressed.

***

When he reached the livery, Otto had the body on the back of the buckboard and the Tobiano saddled for him.

"I expected you sooner," the big man said.

"I got tied up."

"Still," Otto said, "it's only nine. You should be in Goodwill by noon."

"Was Owens the only law?" Clint asked.

"He was," Otto said. "No deputies."

"Does Goodwill have a mayor?"

"Yeah, it does. You'd best take the body to the undertaker, then talk to the mayor. You'll wanna do all that before you tell his wife and child."

"Yeah," Clint said. He tied the Tobiano's reins to the back of the buckboard, then climbed aboard. The body, still wrapped in a blanket, was covered by a second one.

"I don't envy you this job," Otto said. "Not at Christmas, anyway."

"Not at Christmas," Clint said, "or any time."

Chapter Twelve

The going was slow because of snow on the ground, and the buckboard Otto had given him was rickety. Several times he was afraid the wheels were going to come off, but in the end, he made it to Goodwill. Riding down the main street, he saw what the bartender had meant. As decked out as Buckley was for Christmas, the town of Goodwill looked as if Christmas had exploded all over it.

The first thing Clint looked for was the undertaker's office. When he found it, he stopped out front and went inside. A man approached him immediately, smiling broadly, looking nothing like an undertaker. He looked more like . . . an elf. He came out of a back room from where Clint had heard hammering.

"And what can I do for you this holiday season, sir?" the man asked. "Have we lost a loved one?"

"Not a loved one," Clint said. "Not even a friend. I'm afraid it's your sheriff."

The man's smile vanished.

"I'm sorry?"

"Sheriff Owens? He's the sheriff here, isn't he? Or wasn't he?"

"He . . . was?"

"Yes," Clint said, "he's dead now. Can you bring him inside?"

"Yes, yes, of course," the undertaker said. "Let me get my man."

He returned to the back room, came out with a large, dour looking man.

"Where is he?" the man growled.

"Outside, on the buckboard," Clint replied.

"Come out and help me."

They went out together, dragged the blanket-wrapped body off the buckboard and into the office.

"Through there," the undertaker said, pointing to the doorway to the back room.

Clint and the other man carried the sheriff's body back there and placed it on a long wooden table.

"Okay, Elijah," the undertaker said. "You can go back to work."

Elijah nodded and went out a back door. In minutes the hammering started again.

"He's making coffins, I'm afraid," the undertaker said. "How did the poor man die?"

"He was shot by two killers he was trailing," Clint said.

"And what happened to them?"

"I killed them."

"Well, good." The undertaker approached the body and began to unwrap the blanket. Then he stopped and turned to Clint. "I can take care of this. You probably want to tell . . . somebody."

"Yes," Clint said, "his wife and son."

"They live in a house on the edge of town."

"But . . . maybe I should talk to somebody in authority first. Your mayor?"

"City Hall is several blocks up the street. Go another street and you'll find a livery for the buckboard and your horses."

"And what's your name?" Clint asked.

"Elton Standing is my name, sir," the small man said. "As you can see, undertaker."

"Thank you, Mr. Standing."

"Oh," Standing said, as Clint headed for the door, "and your name?"

"Adams," Clint said, "Clint Adams."

When he left Elton Standing, the man's mouth was open.

***

The building with CITY HALL above the door was a small, one-story affair. Clint decided to bypass it and take care of the horses, first. The longer he put off talking to the mayor, the longer he put off talking to the sheriff's wife and son.

"Yeah, I know Otto," the man at the livery said. "I'll take care of his buckboard and horse, and yours. Fine lookin' animal."

"Yes, he is."

"How long will you be in town?" the man asked. "We're celebratin', ya know."

"I can see that," Clint said. "Unfortunately, I brought a body into town, so I'm not doing any celebrating, just yet."

"A shame," the man said. "Well, you probably passed the hotel on the way here. Get yerself settled."

Clint collected his saddlebags and rifle and said, "Thanks, I will."

He walked past City Hall again and approached the Yuletide Hotel. The lobby smelled of pine and eggnog, a drink which Clint hated.

"Good day, sir," the desk clerk greeted. He was a middle-aged man dressed in red-and-green. "Can we help you?"

"I need a room."

"For how long?" the clerk asked, turning the register so Clint could sign it.

"I'm not sure. Maybe a couple of days."

"Perhaps you'll stay with us through Christmas?"

"That's still at least a week or so away," Clint said. "I'll have to see."

"Well, however long you stay," the man said, "welcome." He turned the register back around. "Mr. . . . Adams?"

"That's right," Clint said. "Just give me a small room."

"Yessir."

The clerk handed Clint a key and watched as he went up the stairs.

Chapter Thirteen

Clint looked out the window of his small room. It was dark now, but the street was lit up by candles lining both sides. He knew this was part of their Christmas celebration, but he also knew the town could go up in flames if one candle was knocked over.

The sheriff's wife and son, as well as the town's mayor, needed to be told that Owens was dead, but right at that moment he had no idea how to approach the task. Maybe if he just kept his mouth shut, word would get around from the undertaker. Granted, that was a coward's way out, but he was feeling pretty cowardly about giving the sheriff's family the news.

He should tell the mayor, though, and probably as soon as possible. He doubted the man would be in his office at this time of day. He'd either be having supper somewhere, or he would be home.

Clint left his saddlebags and rifle on the bed and went back down to the lobby. The clerk looked startled by his reappearance.

"Uh, sir?"

"I need to find your mayor," Clint said. "Can you tell me where he lives?"

"Uh, yes, sir."

"How well do you know his habits?"

"Uh, some, but not all."

"Where would he be at this time of day?"

"Probably havin' supper."

"And what about *where* he might be having supper?"

"Uh, there are a couple of places."

"Okay," Clint said, "suppose you start with where his house is, and then tell me those other places he might be . . ."

***

The mayor's house was outside of town, so it would be easier to check where the clerk said the man might be eating his meal. In addition to the locations, he got the clerk to describe the man.

He stopped at one café, didn't see anyone matching the description, then moved to the next one. It was a larger restaurant and was filled with people having their supper. Clint decided just to ask. He grabbed a waiter who was going by as he entered.

"Can you tell me if the mayor is here?" he asked.

"Uh, yes sir," the waiter said. "He's at his usual table."

"Take me to him, please."

"Um, he's eatin', sir."

"That's okay," Clint said. "Just take me."

The waiter led Clint through the restaurant, the interior of which was as festive as the rest of the town. In one corner there was a large Christmas tree with candles and garland on it. Once again, Clint thought about just one of those candles going astray.

They reached a table where a tall man in his fifties, with black hair that came to a widow's peak right between his eyebrows looked up at them.

"Yes?"

"Mr. Mayor," the waiter said, "this man is lookin' for you."

"I'm having my supper," the mayor said to Clint. "Can this wait?"

"No, Mr. Mayor, it can't," Clint said.

The mayor frowned at him. Clint saw that the man had not yet cut into his steak.

"You're a stranger," the mayor said. "Who are you?"

"My name is Clint Adams."

The mayor stared at him, then looked at the waiter and said, "It's all right, Walter." He looked at Clint. "Are you hungry?"

"Actually, I'm starving."

"Bring this man a steak supper," the mayor said to the waiter. "And two beers."

"Yes, sir."

"Have a seat," the mayor said. "Do you mind if I start eating?"

"Go right ahead," Clint said, sitting across from him.

"Tell me," the mayor said, "what brings the Gunsmith to Goodwill, and why are you looking for me?"

"It's about your sheriff, Mr. Mayor."

"Matt Owens? What about him? He's out tracking some killers, right now."

"He found them."

"And?"

"They killed him," Clint said. "I've brought his body back for his family."

The mayor stared at Clint with a piece of steak on his fork, halfway to his mouth.

"Matt Owens is dead?" he asked, and then popped the steak into his mouth.

"That's right."

"How did you happen to get his body?"

"He recruited me when we met in Buckley," Clint said. "I agreed to help him track those killers you mentioned. But they split up, so we did, too. I found him shot to death and lashed to a tree."

"What did you do then, Mr. Adams?" the mayor asked.

"I tracked the men who killed him. I killed them, and then brought him home."

The mayor stared at his plate and chewed what was in his mouth, then sat back, wiping his mouth on a white napkin.

"This is terrible," he said. "The sheriff was a good man."

"Yes, he was," Clint said.

"His wife will have to be told," the mayor said. "Good God, his son . . . and it's Christmas . . ."

The mayor cut into his steak again. It seemed the death of the sheriff had not affected his appetite.

"Mr. Adams, did the sheriff deputize you?"

"No."

"Then why did you help him?"

"He asked me to help him get back to his son Joey by Christmas."

"Well," the mayor said, "it seems like you've done that."

The waiter reappeared and set a steaming plate in front of Clint.

"Go ahead and eat," the mayor said, "and we can figure out how to tell her."

Clint didn't like the mayor, but he was too hungry to do anything but eat.

Chapter Fourteen

The two men ate and discussed how Mrs. Owens should be told of her husband's death. Clint still didn't think the mayor was reacting properly to the demise of the lawman, but the man did offer to take the news to the widow.

"I appreciate that, Mr. Mayor," Clint said, "but I think I should be the one to tell her. After all, I saw him last."

"That sounds reasonable, Mr. Adams," the mayor said. "And by the way, my name is Edgewater, Mayor David Edgewater."

"If you don't mind me saying so," Clint said, "losing your sheriff hasn't seemed to cause you to lose your appetite."

"The sheriff and I were not great friends," the mayor said. "I'm sorry he's dead, but we had our differences and I notice *your* appetite is pretty healthy."

"I was very hungry when I got here," Clint said, "but good point."

"Look," Mayor Edgewater said, "it's a sad thing, there's no denying it. Especially having to tell a widow and her son the news right near Christmas."

"What if we didn't."

"What? Not tell them?"

"I mean, until after Christmas," Clint said. "What if we wait until after Christmas?"

"Will that make it easier?" Edgewater asked.

"Maybe."

"On them, or on you?" the mayor asked.

"I don't know," Clint said. "Maybe both. Maybe neither."

The mayor sat back.

"I'm going to let you decide," he said. "You can go and see her—and the boy—and make your decision."

"That may be best," Clint said.

They finished their meals and the mayor said, "How about some coffee?"

"Yeah, that would be good," Clint said.

The mayor waved to the waiter.

"Coffee and pie," he said.

"Yessir."

"They only have apple today," Edgewater told Clint.

"That's fine."

They had their pie and coffee, and then they left the restaurant together. Clint noticed that the mayor didn't pay.

Outside Edgewater said, "Did you get a hotel room?"

"Yes," Clint said, "at the Yuletide."

The mayor shook his head.

"Stupid name for a hotel, I know," he said. "I'll see to it that you're not charged for the room."

Clint didn't argue.

"I'll walk back with you," he said. "My house is in that direction."

They started walking.

"Is the sheriff at the undertaker's?"

"Yes."

"I was wondering," the mayor said, "did you bring back his badge?"

"It's still on him," Clint said, "where it belongs."

"I'll have to get it," the mayor said. "And I'll need to name a new sheriff. I don't suppose you'd be interested in the job?"

"No thanks," Clint said.

"Just thought I'd ask," the mayor said.

They reached the Yuletide Hotel.

"Aren't you worried these candles might start a fire?" Clint asked, looking up and down the street.

"It's been discussed," the mayor admitted. "We keep the volunteer fire department on alert during Christmas."

"That's good to know."

"Why don't you come to my office in the morning?" the mayor said. "After you have breakfast. We can talk again and see if one of us has come up with . . . something else."

"Okay," Clint said.

"Good-night, Mr. Adams," the mayor said. "I'll see to the sheriff's body. Thank you for bringing him back."

"It's what he deserves," Clint said, and went into the hotel.

Chapter Fifteen

In the morning, Clint had breakfast in the hotel, then walked over to City Hall. Outside the mayor's office sat a middle-aged woman with a no-nonsense demeanor to her.

"Can I help you?" she asked.

"I'm here to see the mayor."

"Is he expecting you?"

"He is."

"That's odd," she said. "He didn't tell me, and I'm his assistant."

"Miss . . .?"

"Mrs. Babcock is my name."

"Mrs. Babcock, I'm sure if you check with him, you'll see that I'm expected. The mayor and I met last night."

"Wait here, please."

She went into the mayor's office, then came out, obviously not pleased.

"The mayor is waiting for you."

"Thank you."

"Coffee?" he asked as Clint entered.

"Please," Clint said.

They sat at the mayor's desk with their cups.

"Any new ideas about how to handle this?" Edgewater asked.

"Not really," Clint said. "They have to be told. It's just a matter of when."

"And that you'll decide," Edgewater said. "Her name is Juliet, and her son is Joey."

"Where do they live?"

"A small house on the outside of town," the mayor said. "But she has a job in town, and the boy attends school."

"Okay," Clint said, "give me directions to their house, where she works, and the school. I'll find an excuse to meet them."

"It shouldn't be hard," the mayor said. "She works at the mercantile store."

"That's good," Clint said. "I guess I'll go and do some shopping."

***

The mercantile was right in the center of town. Clint remembered driving by with the sheriff's body on the back of the buckboard. It seemed ironic, now that he knew the sheriff's wife worked there.

He walked from City Hall to the store and stopped just outside. He thought he would walk right in, but now that he was there, he was losing his nerve. He thought maybe he should walk to the school, but he had even less nerve to see the boy at that moment. No, he had to go into the mercantile and at least get the meeting over with.

He took a deep breath and entered.

The mayor had told him that Juliet Owens was usually the clerk there. Clint saw an impossibly lovely woman in her thirties behind the counter. When she saw him, she smiled in a friendly way, and the smile broke his heart because he knew, at some point, he was going to be the reason that smile went away.

"Can I help you with somethin', sir?" she asked.

"I'm a stranger in town," Clint said. "I just need a few things."

"Well, I'm sure we have most of what you need. Why don't you just tell me, and I'll see what I can do."

Clint found himself buying a new shirt, some coffee, canned peaches, a bag of hard candies and a few other items he had absolutely no use for.

"Is that all?" she asked.

"I think so."

"It looks like you needed more than you thought," she said.

"I suppose I did."

"Some of these things don't exactly go together," she commented, "but let me add everything up for you."

While she did so, he said, "This town looks like it really does Christmas up right."

She smiled while doing her figures.

"Yes, we like the holiday quite a bit."

"We?" he asked.

"My family."

"Oh?" he said. "How big a family?"

"Just me, my husband, and our son," she said.

"A young boy?" he asked.

She nodded. "He's five."

"He must be looking forward to Christmas," Clint said.

"Oh, he is," she said, "and he's looking forward to his father coming home, although I doubt that's going to happen."

"Oh, why's that?"

She didn't look up from what she was doing.

"Oh, he's off gallivanting around the countryside," she said.

"What's he do?" Clint asked.

"He's the sheriff," she said. "He's off chasing out-laws, of course, even though he knows it's Christmas and his son wants him home."

"And you?" Clint asked. "Don't you want your husband home for the holidays?"

"Actually," she said, "I really don't care." She looked up at him then and smiled. "Why all the questions?"

"Well, uh, I, uh—" he stammered.

"Are you trying to find out if it's all right to flirt with me?"

"What?" he asked. "Oh, no, I wouldn't—"

"Because it is, you know," she said, handing him his check. "Do you want to pay for this now?"

"Oh," he said, "sure." He reached into his pocket for his money.

Chapter Sixteen

When Clint left the mercantile, he walked to the schoolhouse. He looked in the window and saw a woman standing up in front of about a dozen kids. There seemed to be an even number of boys and girls, running in age from five to about twelve. Only three looked about five years old, and two of them were girls. Joey Owens must have been the boy sitting in a front seat.

The inside and outside of the schoolhouse were decorated for Christmas. He couldn't hear what the teacher was saying but thought he could crack the window open a bit without alerting anyone. Once that was done, he could hear what she was saying. She was pointing to some words on the blackboard, wanting the smaller children to read them aloud.

"Come on, Joey," she said to the boy, "you can do it."

And that was how Clint *knew* he was looking at Joey Owens. The boy seemed to stare at the blackboard like it was something foreign to him, and then he said, "I can't."

"Sure you can, Joey," the teacher said. "You know these words."

"I can't, I can't," he snapped, and then suddenly he was up from his desk and running. Clint heard the schoolhouse door slam open. The teacher ran to the door and shouted, "Joseph Owens, you come back here!"

But the boy kept running. When the teacher went back inside, Clint followed the small boy's tracks. He found him sitting on a fallen tree with his chin in his hands, his elbows on his knees, staring straight again. Clint circled around so that he could approach him from the other side, as if it was accidental.

As he approached, the boy looked up. His eyes went wide for a moment, but when he saw Clint, he seemed to calm down. He was probably relieved it wasn't his teacher or his mother.

"Hi there," Clint said.

"Hello."

"What are you doing out here without a coat?" he asked.

"Nothin'."

Clint walked over and stood in front of him.

"You mind if I sit?"

Joey shrugged.

"I tell you what," Clint said, removing his jacket. "I'll sit next to you, and you can wear this so you don't freeze."

Joey shrugged as Clint placed his jacket on the small boy's shoulders.

"So," Clint said, "what are you doing out here on a school day?"

The boy shrugged.

"Come on," Clint said, "you can do more than shrug. Be a man and tell me what's going on."

The boy looked at him.

"Why should I tell you?" he asked.

"Why not?" Clint said. "We're both out here in the cold. We might as well talk."

Joey stared straight ahead again, but then he started to speak.

"I ran out of school," he said.

"Why would you do that?"

"Because the teacher wanted me to read some stupid words off the blackboard," the boy said.

"And you didn't want to?"

"No!"

"Why?"

"Because it's stupid!"

"The words on the board?" Clint asked. "Or school in general?"

"Everythin'!"

"I get the feeling this is about something other than school," Clint said.

Joey clamped his mouth shut and firmed his chin.

"Maybe we should go and find your pa and see what he thinks."

"My father's not here!" Joey snapped.

"Oh? Where is he?"

"I dunno! He's out doin' his stupid job!"

"And what would that be?"

"He's the sheriff."

"Really?" Clint said. "Well, you must be real proud of him, then."

"I'm not proud," Joey said. "I'm mad."

"At your father?"

The boy nodded.

"Why's that?"

"Because he ain't here, and it's almost Christmas," Joey said. "He's supposed to be here for Christmas."

"Well, there's still time," Clint said, feeling like a total bastard.

"Naw, he ain't comin'," Joey said. "He thinks his stupid, stupid job is more important than me."

"What about your mother?"

"She don't care."

"I'm sure she cares about you and loves you," Clint said.

"She don't care about my father," Joey said.

"Why do you say that?"

"Because before he left, they was fightin' the whole time."

"About what?"

"I dunno," Joey said. "Everythin'. They didn't agree on nothin'." Joey turned his head and looked at Clint. "Do you know what a divorce is?"

"Uh, well, yeah, I do."

"I think they're gettin' a divorce."

He looked forward again, chin in his hands.

"How do you know what a divorce is?" Clint asked.

"Judy told me," he said.

"Who's Judy?"

"My girlfriend," Joey said. "She's twelve."

"You have a twelve-year-old girlfriend?"

"Yeah, I do."

"How old are you?"

"Five."

"What makes you think Judy's your girlfriend?"

"She tells me all the time," Joey said.

"And where's Judy now?"

"She's in school," he said. "She sits in the back be-cause she's one of the oldest. I sit in front 'cause I'm the littlest. But she says I'm cute, and that's why I'm her boyfriend."

It sounded to Clint like the girl was being nice to the little boy.

"Joey," he said, "my name's Clint." He took the bag he'd bought at the mercantile from his pocket. "You want some candy?"

Chapter Seventeen

Rather than take Joey back to the schoolhouse, Clint decided to bring the boy to his mother. Maybe he could find out what was going on between the sheriff and his wife before he gave the family the bad news.

Joey agreed to go, so they started to walk, but part of the way there the boy started to slow down.

"You want a lift?" Clint asked, and picked the boy up before he could answer.

"You don't live in town," Joey said. "I ain't never seen you before."

"I just got to town yesterday."

"Are you a gunfighter?" Joey asked.

"Why would you ask that?"

"'cause you look like a gunfighter."

"What does a gunfighter look like?"

"I dunno," Joey said, shrugging, "a gunfighter."

"Well, you think about it," Clint said, "and when you can tell me what a gunfighter looks like, I'll tell you if I am one."

The boy gave that some thought, then said, "You got anymore candy?"

"Sure," Clint said, "but you better finish eating it before we find your mother."

***

When Clint reached the mercantile, he put Joey down and started to reclaim his jacket, but the boy ran into the store, half dragging it with him.

"Joey!" Clint heard Juliet Owens snap. "What are you doin' out of school? And whose jacket is that?"

"It's Clint's," Joey said. "He gave it to me so I wouldn't freeze."

"Who's Clint?" she asked, as Clint stepped through the door.

"That would be me," he said.

"You?" she said, recognizing him. "What were you doin' with my son? Why's he out of school?"

"I don't know," Clint said. "I found him sitting on a log, freezing. So I gave him my jacket and brought him here."

"I—well, that was very nice of you," she said. "Joey, give the man back his jacket."

"He's Clint," Joey said. "His name's Clint." He turned and handed Clint his jacket, then looked back at his mother. "I think he's a gunfighter."

"Did he tell you that?" she asked.

"Well, no . . . but I think it. He wouldn't tell me."

"I don't think that's the kind of thing you ask somebody," she said, "especially a stranger."

"But he ain't a stranger," Joey insisted, "he's Clint. He's my friend. He gave me candy."

"Oh, he did?"

"Just a piece or two," Clint said. "I bought it from you."

"So you did." She looked at her son. "You and me, we're gonna have a talk about you leavin' school."

"Aw, Ma," Joey said, "school's stupid."

"If you don't go to school," Clint said, "you'll be the one who's stupid."

"See? Even Clint knows you have to go to school."

"Aw, Ma—"

"You go in the back room and find somethin' to do," she said. "We'll be goin' home soon."

"Yes, Ma. Bye, Clint. Thanks for the candy."

"You're welcome, Joey."

The little boy went through the doorway to the back room.

"I'm sorry if he was any trouble," she said. "He should be in school."

"Don't be too hard on him," Clint suggested. "He's having a hard time with something."

"Oh? Did he say what?"

"Well . . . it's not really something I should get involved with," Clint said. "It's . . . personal."

She folded her arms and said, "I think I know what it is. Did you discuss it with him?"

"I didn't," Clint said. "I didn't think it was my place."

"Well, thank you for that," she said. "I have enough people trying to tell me how to handle my son."

"It seems everybody's an expert," Clint said.

"Wow, you said it!"

They both laughed.

"Well, I'll be going," Clint said. "You wouldn't know a good place in town to have supper, would you?" It was out of his mouth before he even knew it.

"Yes, I do," she said. "My house."

"Oh hey, I didn't mean—"

"Never mind," she said. "You kept my son from freezin'. That's at least worth a home cooked meal."

"That does sound good," Clint admitted.

"I'll give you directions," she said, "and you can come by at seven."

He smiled. "I'll be there."

Chapter Eighteen

He followed Juliet's directions and got to the small house on the edge of town by five minutes to seven.

When she opened the door he said, "I hope I'm not too early."

"Right on time," she said. "Come in."

He entered the house, found it warm and cozy. It was also decorated for Christmas, but not as over-the-top as the rest of the town. And there was no tree.

"Have a seat at the table," she said. "Dinner's almost ready."

He sat and swiveled his head around.

"Where's your Christmas tree?" he asked.

"My husband usually goes out and cuts one down," she said. "But as you know, he's not here."

"Well, you can't have Christmas without a tree," he said. "What're you going to put Joey's gifts underneath?"

"That might not be a problem," Juliet said. "Unless I sneak some gifts out of the store, which would be stealin'."

"Won't your boss extend you some credit?" he asked.

"Not anymore."

"What about the town?" Clint asked. "Won't they give you some of your husband's pay?"

"No," she said, "they only give him his pay."

"Then how are you living, Juliet?" he asked.

She turned her back to the stove and looked at him. He looked at her. She appeared very fetching in a yellow dress that showed off her figure.

"Day to day," she said, "we're livin' day to day . . . Clint? Is that what Joey said your name was?"

"That's right," he said. "Clint."

"He likes you," she said.

"Of course he does," Clint said. "I gave him candy."

"Your candy, right?" she asked. "You bought that candy for yourself, didn't you?"

"I did," he said. "I have a sweet tooth."

"Well then, it was nice of you to give him your candy and your jacket."

She turned back to the stove, looked into the pots and pans and then yelled, "Joey, supper! Clint's here."

The boy came running in from another room of the house.

"Hi, Clint!" he yelled, stopping just short of bumping into him.

"Hey, Joey."

"Young man," his mother said, "you come over here to the sink and wash those hands."

"Yes, ma'am."

As he trudged over to the sink, Juliet looked at Clint and said, "You, too."

"Yes, Ma'am," Clint said, standing up.

***

Supper was both succulent and opulent, and he felt bad that she had used so much of her supplies to make it for him. It looked as if she had tossed every vegetable and bit of meat she had into the stew. He was going to have to do something to help her.

And he was also going to have to tell her that her husband was dead. He had probably made a mistake meeting both Juliet and her son. Now he felt even worse that he was going to have to give them the bad news.

Hearing that his father was dead was going to break Joey's heart. And even though Juliet and the sheriff had been having problems, it wasn't going to be easy for her to hear.

While they ate, he watched mother and son laugh and enjoy what they had. The boy deserved to have a good Christmas, even though his daddy was dead. Clint just had to figure out how to give them a good holiday.

One way came to mind.

"Hey, Joey," he said, "tomorrow's Saturday. Why don't we go out and cut down a tree."

Chapter Nineteen

"I can't ask you to do that," Juliet said.

"You didn't ask me," Clint said. "I offered."

"Ma!" Joey plcaded. "We need a tree. Pleeeze?"

"Yes," Clint said, "please?"

"Well," Juliet said, "all right. I don't suppose I can argue with you both."

***

After supper, Juliet told Joey to say goodnight to Clint and then put him to bed.

"I'll get going," he offered.

"No," she said, "wait. We'll have coffee and a slice of a cobbler I made today."

"That's an offer I can't resist," he said.

"I'll be right back."

While she was in the other room with Joey, Clint looked around. He assumed that everything in the house was a reflection of her tastes, and not Sheriff Owens'. He also assumed she had probably decorated the house by herself or with Joey's help.

"He's finally down," she said, returning to the room. "I swear, he wears me out."

"Isn't that his job?" Clint asked.

She laughed.

"Yes, I suppose it is," she said. "I'm having a sliver of pie. How about you? Sliver or large slice?"

"Oh, definitely large," he said.

"Have a seat," she said. "I'll bring it right over."

Clint sat back at the table, and she brought them a pot of coffee and two pieces of peach cobbler.

"I make my peach cobblers with cinnamon," she said. "I hope you don't mind."

"That sounds delicious," Clint said. "Peach happens to be my favorite."

She poured them each a cup of coffee.

"You know," she said, "you really don't have to take Joey out to cut down a tree tomorrow."

"Oh, I don't dare disappoint him now," Clint said. "I said I'd do it, and I will. We'll find a really nice one."

He cut off a hunk of the cobbler and stuck it in his mouth. "This is amazing!" he said as he chewed.

"Thank you."

After the pie and coffee, she walked him outside.

"I'll be back early to take Joey out," he promised.

"Not too early, I hope," she said. "I'm going into the store a little later tomorrow."

"Why?"

"Mr. Turner, the owner, told me I've been looking tired lately and I should get more sleep. I guess he doesn't want me to scare off the customers with dark circles under my eyes."

"You look fine to me," he said.

"Thank you, but a little extra sleep tomorrow wouldn't hurt."

"You've got it," Clint said. "I'll come by around ten."

"Ten would be good," she said. "Thank you, Clint."

"Good-night, Juliet. Thanks for the home cooked meal."

He started walking back toward town.

***

After Clint left, Juliet was cleaning up when Joey came out, rubbing his eyes.

"Where's Clint?" he asked.

"He left," she said. "What are you doin' up, young man?"

"I thought I heard Pa."

"No, Joey," she said, "it must have been a dream."

She sat down and he came over to lean on her. She put her arm around him.

"Pa's not comin' home, is he, Ma?"

"Joey," She said, "if he can come home, he will."

"For Christmas?" Joey asked.

"If he can."

"Why won't he be able to?" the boy asked.

"Well, Joey, your father is the sheriff," she said. "He has a job to do, and he won't be able to come home until he's done it."

"Chasing bad men?" the boy asked.

"Yes, chasing bad men."

"But what if—"

"Joey," she said, "I think you better go to bed now, young man. You want to be ready in the morning when Clint gets here to take you for a tree."

He started for the bedroom, then stopped and turned. "Will Clint really come to take me out to cut down a Christmas tree, Ma?"

"Yes, Joey," she said, "Clint will definitely really be here."

"'night, Ma," he said, and ran to bed.

Juliet put her elbows on the table, and her head in her hands. She was hoping that Clint wouldn't be another man who was going to disappoint Joey with a promise he didn't keep.

Chapter Twenty

As promised, Clint did not appear at the Owens house early the next morning. Instead, he stopped at the mercantile. As he entered, he assumed the older man behind the counter was Juliet's boss. He bought a small carton of groceries, without telling the man who they were for, as well as an axe. Then he carried his purchases to Juliet and Joey's house, arriving at five minutes to ten.

"What's this?" Juliet asked, as she opened the door.

"I felt bad about eating all your food last night," Clint said, "so I thought I'd pick up a few things." He walked in, put the carton down on the table, then reached inside. "Including a bag of hard candy for Joey. Where is he?"

"He's gettin' dressed," she said, looking through the carton. "Clint, you didn't have to do all this."

"Hey," he said, "can I help it if being in this town has given me the holiday spirit?"

"Yes, but—"

"Clint!" Joey yelled, running into the room. "You came back."

"I told you I'd be here," Clint said. "Are you ready to hunt for a tree?"

"Yeaaaaahh!"

"Not without a jacket, young man," Juliet said. "Come on."

"Aw, Ma . . ."

She put the boy's jacket on him and wrapped a scarf around his neck.

"There, now you'll be warm," she told him.

"Let's go, Joey," Clint said, heading for the door with the axe in hand.

"The door will be unlocked so you can bring the tree in," Juliet told him. "I've cleared away that corner for it." She pointed

"You got it," Clint said.

"And when you're finished, could you bring Joey to the store? I'll keep him there with me the rest of the day."

"Don't worry about a thing," Clint said. "Joey and I are going to have lunch together after we get the tree, then I'll bring him to the store."

"Clint, you don't have to—"

"Hey," Clint said, putting his arm around the boy, "me and my buddy are going to be hungry after chopping down a tree . . . right Joey?"

"Right!"

Clint and Joey went out the door and headed for the woods. Juliet watched them trudge away through the snow, a tear in her eye. She hadn't seen her boy this happy in a long while.

***

Clint allowed Joey to take the lead, and the boy kept running up to trees, pointing and yelling, "That one? That one?"

"No," Clint said, calmly. "Keep walking."

As they walked along, Joey asked, "So, are you gonna tell me?"

"Tell you what?"

"If you're a gunfighter."

"Can you tell me what a gunfighter looks like?" Clint asked.

"Sure."

"What?"

Joey smiled up at him.

"He looks like you," the boy said.

"You're a smartass," Clint said.

"That's a bad word."

"But accurate."

"What's accurate?" Joey asked, trotting to keep just ahead of Clint.

"That means it's correct."

"I'm gonna tell my ma—"

Clint stopped walking.

"If you want a tree, don't threaten me with your mother," he said.

Joey looked ashamed and said, "A-all right."

"Let's keep walking."

As they started up again, Joey said, "My pa told me that gunfighters wear their guns like it's part of them. That's what you do, Clint."

Clint stopped walking.

"What is it?" Joey asked.

Clint pointed and said, "That one. It's a Noble Fir and will last the longest."

Joey turned and looked at the tree Clint was pointing to.

"It's big," he said.

"Yes," Clint said, "after we cut it down, we'll have to drag it to the house."

"Can we do that?" Joey asked.

Clint hefted the axe and said, "We're going to find out."

***

After Joey watched Clint chop the tree down, and it had come crashing to the ground, he ran to it, grabbed the trunk and started pulling.

"It's heavy," he said.

"You're right," Clint said. "We'll have to go back to the livery and get my horse. He'll be able to drag it."

"Can I ride 'im?" Joey asked, excitedly.

Clint ruffled the young boy's hair and said, "Sure, why not?"

Chapter Twenty-One

Clint and Joey walked back to the livery, where Clint put the bridle and saddle on the Tobiano. They then walked back to where the downed tree was. Clint tied a rope to the tree, and to the saddle, so the Tobiano could drag it back to the house.

"Okay, Joey, up you go." Clint lifted Joey up into the saddle, but knew he'd have to walk alongside to keep the boy from falling off. It would have been easier just to have him walk, but the boy was excited to ride.

Clint had to struggle with the heavy tree to get it through the door. He moved some furniture aside so he could drag it over to the corner Juliet had chosen for it. That done, he and Joey went back outside to the barn, where Clint found some pieces of wood and tools that he could use to build a stand for the tree so that it would stand up straight.

It didn't take long. Clint hadn't really made a tree stand before, but he had seen it done. He thought he had it right and carried it back to the house.

"This is the biggest tree we ever had," Joey said. "Is it gonna stand up?"

"I hope so, Joey," Clint said. "I really hope so."

The boy was too small to be of any real help, so Clint had to struggle to prop the tree up once he attached the stand to the bottom. It turned out to be too high for the ceiling, so he had to lay it down again and trim it. This time when he got it into standing position, it fit. He and Joey backed away to admire their work.

"It's stayin'," Joey said, excitedly.

"Yeah," Clint said, "but I want to make sure."

They went back to the barn, where Clint found some twine, nails and a hammer. Back at the house, he tied the twine to the tree, hammered nails in the wall and twisted the twine around them. This would make sure that the tree remained upright.

"There we go," Clint said. "Now you and your mama can decorate it."

"You, too," Joey insisted. "You can help us decorate it."

"I don't know, Joey," Clint said. "Maybe your pa will come home, and he can do it."

"He ain't comin'," Joey said.

"Why do you say that?"

"Mama don't want him to."

"Did she say that?"

Joey shook his head.

"But I know," he said.

Clint ruffled the boy's hair.

"Come on, let's see if we can rustle up some lunch," he said.

"You can cook?" Joey asked.

"Sure I can cook."

"Potatoes?"

"Sure, I can make potatoes," Clint said. "How do you want them?"

"Any way," Joey said, happily. "I like potatoes cooked any way."

"Well then, let's see what your ma's got in your root cellar."

"Oh boy," Joey said. "It's over here." He grabbed Clint's hand and tugged him over to the entrance of the root cellar. "Clint?"

"Yeah?"

"You got any more candy?"

"Yeah," Clint said, "I've got a few more pieces for you, buddy."

***

Clint didn't feel bad about raiding the root cellar, since he had brought some groceries with him that morning. He found a hunk of ham that Juliet had salted to preserve it and made himself and Joey some sandwiches. He then resalted what was left and put it back.

Once they finished eating, Clint decided to take Joey to the mercantile and leave him with his mother.

"Come on, Joey," he said. "We're going to town."

"Can I ride Toby?" the boy asked.

"Sure you can. We both can."

He took Joey outside, put him in the saddle, then climbed up behind him. Then he turned the Tobiano and they rode for town.

**

When they reached town, he reined in the Tobiano in front of the store, dismounted and took Joey down. The boy's feet barely touched the ground when he started running into the store.

"Ma! Ma! We put the tree up!"

Juliet got down on her knees and hugged her little boy to her, then tossed a murderous look at Clint over the boy's shoulder. The bottom fell out of his stomach.

She knew.

Chapter Twenty-Two

Juliet hugged Joey tightly, then said, "Go on into the back room, Joey. I'll be right there."

"Okay, Ma."

The boy ran off.

Juliet stood, walked to Clint, slapped his face and asked, "When were you going to tell me?"

"I—I don't know," he said. "I'm sorry, but I didn't know how. And I didn't want to spoil Joey's Christmas."

"What happened?"

"How'd you find out?"

"The undertaker came in, asked when I wanted to bury my husband."

"I'm so sorry, Juliet."

"What happened to him? How did you meet him?"

Clint looked at the door to the back room, afraid Joey might come back in. Or maybe he was standing there, listening to them.

"Let's go out front," he suggested. He tried to take her arm, but she pulled away from him.

When they got outside, he told her how he had met Matt Owens, and agreed to help him. And then he told her what happened.

She stared off into space for a few moments, then wiped a single tear away as it rolled down her cheek.

"He shouldn't have involved you," she said, finally. "It wasn't fair."

"He was trying to get back here for Joey."

"Joey always came second to his job," she said.

"And you?"

"Me? I was way down the list." She folded her arms. "I suppose if he hadn't asked you for help, I still wouldn't know what happened to him."

"Not until somebody found him," Clint said.

She turned and looked over her shoulder.

"And you're probably right about tellin' Joey," she said. "I want him to have a good Christmas."

"He's happy with the tree."

"I suppose I should thank you for that," she said, "now that I know Matt's not comin' back."

"No need—"

"I can't talk to you anymore right now, Clint," she said. "I need some time."

"I understand."

"Thank you for bringin' Joey to me," she said, then turned, went back into the store and closed the door.

***

Juliet stood next to the counter for a few moments, collecting herself. Then went into the back room to see her son. He was sitting at a small desk she had put there for him, drawing.

"Look Ma," he said, holding up the picture. "It's the tree me and Clint cut down. We're gonna decorate it. Can Clint decorate it with us?"

"I don't think so, Joey," she said. "Clint has things to do."

"But he said he would."

"Well then, I guess we'll just have to see," she said. Joey frowned.

"Did you tell him he can't come?" he asked. "Because of Pa?"

"No, Joey," she said, "I didn't tell him he couldn't come."

"Then he will," Joey said. "He'll come and help us decorate. He said so. Because he ain't Pa."

"No," Juliet said, "he's not."

***

Clint went to Mayor Edgewater's office. Mrs. Babcock let him go right in.

"What can I do for you?" the mayor asked.

"You can tell me why your undertaker went to Juliet Owens and told her about her dead husband."

"I know, I heard about that," the mayor said, sitting back in his chair. "I'm sorry, I don't think he understood—"

"Is he going to tell the boy, too?"

"No," the mayor said, "he'll leave that to the boy's mother."

"I hope so," Clint said.

"What are you going to do?" the mayor asked. "Leave town now that she knows?"

"I'm not sure," Clint said. "I might stay a while."

"Why?"

"Hey," Clint said, "it's almost Christmas. I might as well be here than out on the trail somewhere, wandering, like the three wise men."

"They weren't wandering," Edgewater said. "They were heading for Jerusalem the whole time."

"Yeah, well, I wasn't heading here the whole time," Clint said, "but I'm here now."

Chapter Twenty-Three

Clint wasn't at all sure what was keeping him in Goodwill now. Was it the boy? The woman? The dead sheriff? Or was it Christmas?

He didn't go back to the store. He was sure Juliet wouldn't want him there. But he didn't want Joey to think he'd abandoned him. He already thought that about his father.

He decided to go to his hotel, freshen up, maybe even have a bath. Then he could get a drink and a meal, and just settle down and think.

***

After his bath, he stepped out of the hotel in fresh clothes, feeling clean and refreshed, but still frustrated. He wished he'd told Juliet about her husband, instead of finding out the way she did.

He saw a saloon called The High Spade across the street and walked over to it. It was still early, and there wasn't much activity inside. In addition to the bartender, there were two girls, a blonde and a brunette, sitting at a table together, waiting for customers.

"Ladies," he said.

"Lookin' for company, handsome?" the brunette asked.

"Just a beer, thanks."

"Too bad," the blonde said, and the two girls laughed. Neither of them looked to have hit thirty, yet.

He walked to the bar, where a tall, thin bartender waited.

"Beer, please," Clint said.

"Comin' up."

The bartender drew a cold beer and set it in front of him. Clint looked around at the sparse Christmas decorations.

"It's not as overboard in here as the rest of the town," Clint said.

"I'm lazy," the bartender said. "The girls do it, little by little. By the time we get to Christmas Eve, it'll be different."

"I see." Clint sipped the cold beer.

"You're a stranger in town," the bartender said. "This must be . . . weird for you."

"It's . . . a lot to take in, that's for sure," Clint said. "But I'm sure it makes the people in this town happy."

"Oh, it does," the bartender said. "The celebrations will start soon. Parties for children, for adults, all leading up to a big one on Christmas Eve."

The brunette got up from the table, walked over and leaned on the bar next to him.

"You should stick around for that one," she said. "It's usually a lot of fun."

"I'm thinking about it."

"Well, while you're thinkin' about it, how about buyin' me a drink?"

"Give the lady what she wants," Clint told the bartender. "And the other one, too."

"I'm Candy," the brunette said, "and that's Velvet."

"Come on over and have a drink, Velvet," Clint invited.

"Champagne for both the ladies," the bartender said.

"And give them the real stuff," Clint told the man. "Not the watered-down version."

"You're the boss," the bartender said.

Velvet came over, and now Clint had a girl on either side of him . . .

***

Two hours later he still had a girl on either side of him, only they were naked and asleep . . .

***

After a few glasses of champagne, the girls had invited him upstairs.

"There's nothin' goin' on down here," Candy said.

"Won't be for a while," Velvet said, putting her hand on his arm. "Nobody will miss us."

"It sounds tempting—" Clint started, but Candy knew where he was going and cut him off.

"No charge," she said.

Clint looked at the bartender.

"Hey," the man said, "it's up to them. I'm no pimp."

"Come on," Candy said, "it's Christmas. Let us give you an early present."

"And you can give us one." Velvet laughed.

"Well," Clint said, "when you put it that way . . ."

"And another bottle of champagne," Candy said, looking at the bartender. "On the house."

"You girls are killin' me," the bartender said. "Okay, here ya go." He handed the brunette a bottle.

The girls walked on either side of Clint, who kept his gun arm free just in case. But they went right to the stairs and up to a room with—surprise, surprise—Christmas decorations and a clean bed.

In minutes, both girls had shucked their dresses and stood naked in front of Clint. Candy, the brunette, was long and lean, with small breasts, like peaches. Her skin was dark, her nipples brown. Velvet, the blonde, was shorter and full, with pear-shaped breasts. Her skin was very pale, and her nipples pink.

"What are you waitin' for, handsome?" Candy asked.

Clint felt foolish as he said, "I just don't know where to start."

Chapter Twenty-Four

But he figured it out.

He started by removing his gunbelt and hanging it on the bedpost, then divesting himself of all his clothes until he was as naked as they were.

"My, my, Velvet," Candy said, "you ever seen a tallywacker as pretty as that one?"

"Not in all my born days," Velvet answered.

The two naked women approached him, ran their hands over him. He reached for them, but Candy pushed his hands away.

"You just stand there, Mister, and let us enjoy you," she said.

Clint looked over at the locked door and the windows. This was the perfect set-up for a trap, but who would have set him up? Who would have known he was coming to this saloon? No, it appeared the women were exactly what they seemed.

So he stood still and let them roam his body with their hands, running them up and down his legs, over his buttocks, and then finally running their fingertips over the smooth skin of his burgeoning penis.

Eventually they knelt in front of him, fondling his thighs, his balls, then leaned forward and ran their lips over him. His cock swelled to almost bursting, and they the rose, each taking a hand, as they led him to the bed . . .

***

Now it was hours later, and he was pleasantly exhausted. He ran a hand down each of their backs to their buttocks, which he stroked until they woke.

"Jesus," Candy said, "we gotta go back to work."

"Yeah," Velvet said. "Playtime is over."

"What was this all about?" he asked, as they got up and dressed.

"What do you think?" Candy asked, checking her face in the mirror above the dresser.

"Fun," Velvet said. "There was nothing happenin', and we were bored."

"And it's Christmas," Candy said. "Like we said, we all give each other gifts."

Fully dressed, the girls turned and faced the bed.

"You can stay up here as long as you want," Candy said. "It's my room."

"No, that's all right," he said, swinging his feet to the floor. "I'll get dressed and be on my way."

"You come back and see us again, you hear?" Velvet said. "Before you leave town?"

"I might be around til Christmas," he said, starting to dress.

"Good," Candy said, "maybe we can spend Christmas Eve together."

"We'll see," he said. "Ladies . . . thank you for the fun."

"Let's go," Candy said to Velvet. "I can hear them downstairs."

They both waved at him and left the room. He accidently kicked the empty champagne bottle while getting dressed, strapped on his gun, and did the same.

***

Juliet and Joey left the mercantile and she locked the door behind them.

"Are we gonna walk home?" he asked.

"Yup," Juliet said, "that's what I do every day."

"Clint let me ride his horse here," he said. "Maybe he'll let me ride it home?"

"Clint's busy, Joey," she said. "He's gonna be busy for a while."

"Like Pa?"

"No," she said, fighting back a tear, "not like your Pa."

"Then why can't he come with us?" He asked. "We gotta decorate the tree."

"We're gonna do that," she said, as they started to walk. "You and me. We're gonna put garland, and ribbons and candles on it."

"Oh boy! Can we run home, Ma?"

"No," Juliet said, "I'd never be able to keep up with your strong young legs, you rascal." She put an arm around his shoulders. "Let's just walk."

***

Clint saw the girls already sitting with customers as he walked through the saloon. The place was about half full and getting fuller by the minute as men staggered through the doors, looking for fun and entertainment after work.

He stopped at the bar for a last beer, which he drank right down gratefully, then left. He realized that for the time he was with the two girls, he hadn't thought about Juliet and Joey. Now he wondered where they were and what they were doing?

Chapter Twenty-Five

Being with the two girls gave him an appetite. He found a café down the street where he could have a steak. While he ate, he thought about Juliet and Joey. He needed something else to think about. He wondered what the mayor would do about replacing the dead sheriff? He'd offered the job to Clint, but now he would be trying to find somebody else.

Since the undertaker told Juliet about her husband being dead, Clint assumed the news must have gotten around town. It was possible the only one who didn't know about it yet was little Joey.

"Anythin' else, sir?" the old waiter asked.

"Yes," Clint said, "some more bread."

"Right away."

The steak was tough, but edible. The vegetables were done well, and the bread was fresh. The meal was nothing like the home-cooked one Juliet had given him, but it satisfied his hunger.

The waiter brought the extra bread, and it reminded Clint of the scene he'd read in the Dickens book, *A Christmas Carol*. Scrooge asks a waiter for more bread, and the waiter tells him it'll be extra. Scrooge thinks for a second and then says, "No more bread!"

"Will this cost extra?" Clint asked.

"No, sir."

"Thanks."

He felt bad about the way Juliet had heard the news. He should have told her right away. Perhaps then she wouldn't be angry with him, and he would be able to offer her some assistance.

He finished his meal, paid his bill and left the cafe. He wanted to go to Juliet's house, just to show Joey that he hadn't left town, if he was sure Juliet wouldn't shoot him on sight. Maybe tomorrow . . .

He went back to his hotel to his room, found the bread scene in the Dickens book, read it again, and laughed.

***

He stayed in his room the rest of the night, went to bed early. His arms and legs ached from the effort of cutting the tree down, and then setting it up. And he was exhausted from the time he spent with the two girls. So he slept soundly.

He woke the next morning, still sore, and hungry again. He got dressed and went down to the hotel dining room for breakfast. While he was there, he saw Mrs. Babcock come to the entrance of the dining room, look around and then cross the room to him.

"Mr. Adams," she said.

"Mrs. Babcock," he greeted. "Good-morning. Will you join me?"

She hesitated a moment, then said, "Perhaps for a cup of tea."

He waved the waiter over and ordered tea for her.

"I assume you came here looking for me?" he asked.

"I did," she said.

"On behalf of the mayor?"

"On his behalf, but he didn't send me," she said. "I came on my own."

"Why?"

"He needs help."

"What kind of help?"

"He can't find anyone to take the sheriff's job."

"There must be somebody who wants it."

"There's more to it, Mr. Adams," she said. "A gang's in the area. They attack towns that don't have any law."

"So he thinks they'll hear that there's no sheriff here and attack?"

"That's what he's afraid of."

The waiter came and set her tea down in front of her.

"And there's one more thing," she said, stirring cream into her cup.

"More?"

She nodded.

"They like to hit towns on the Jingle Bell Trail."

"I thought the Jingle Bell Trail was between here and Buckley?"

She shook her head.

"It starts at Buckley, comes here and then keeps going north," she said. "There are other towns the gang has hit. They loot, and they kill. Some of the towns recovered from the attacks and now have law."

"But Goodwill has none."

"Right."

"So you want me to wear the badge?"

"I thought, just until the mayor can find someone else."

"And how long do you think that will take?"

"Well . . ."

"Don't tell me there's more to this?"

She sipped her tea and nodded.

"Okay," he said, "give it to me."

Chapter Twenty-Six

At the same moment Mrs. Babcock was having tea with Clint, Mayor David Edgewater was sitting in a meeting of the town council.

"I thought you had this handled, Mayor," Lester Tinsley said.

"So did I," the mayor said. "Sheriff Owens kept that gang out of this town every year he was the law. When I heard he was dead, I thought I'd be able to replace him."

"And you haven't," Tinsley said.

"No."

"What about Clint Adams?" Andy York asked. "Ain't he still in town?"

"He is, but I already asked him."

"Did you tell him about this crazy holiday gang?" Tinsley asked.

"No."

"Why not?"

"Because it sounds mad," Edgewater said. "A gang that only hits on holidays? Come on!"

"We hear about it every year, don't we?" York asked. The other four members of the council nodded.

"That's right, we hear about it," Edgewater asked. "Have any of you ever gone to a town that was hit? No, and neither have I."

"So after all these years you're sayin' you don't believe it," Tinsley accused.

"What about that town they hit on Thanksgiving, just last month?" York said.

"Heller?" Edgewater said.

"Hell-town is more like it," York said. "At least, after the gang hit, it was hell."

"Did you see it?" the mayor asked.

"I ain't seen God, but I believe in him!" York snapped.

"Okay, look," Edgewater said, "I'll try that angle with Adams and see what happens."

"It's Christmas, for chrissake," Tinsley said. "He can't just leave us to the wolves."

"Like I said," Edgewater repeated, "I'll try."

The town council all scraped their chairs back as they stood up.

"You better try hard," Tinsley said.

***

"They only attack on holidays," Mrs. Babcock said. "You're kidding."

114

"I'm not," she said, "The last time was Thanksgiving. They just about burned a town called Heller to the ground."

"They do this all year?" Clint asked.

She nodded.

"Fourth of July we heard they hit a town at the north end of the trail. Ackland, it was called. Supposedly, it doesn't exist, anymore."

"Wait a minute," Clint said, "how do you know all this?"

"We heard it."

"But nobody's ever gone to one of these towns after it's been attacked?"

"Well, no. All we know is that as long as Sheriff Owens was the law here, we didn't have to worry about them."

"Anybody know who the head of this gang is?"

"No."

"How many men they have?"

"No."

"Mrs. Babcock . . ." Clint said, dubiously, "why do I think you're just trying to get me to take that job?"

"Talk to the mayor," she suggested. "He'll tell you all about it."

"I think I'll do that."

She finished her tea and said, "Then I believe I'm done here." She stood up. "Oh, and please don't tell him I was here to see you."

"I won't."

"If you take the job, Mr. Adams," she said before leaving, "you'll save Christmas."

She went walking out with her head high.

***

Clint replayed the conversation in his head over and over again. She said he'd save Christmas. Certainly no pressure there.

He paid his bill, put on his jacket and went out in front of the hotel. It was cold, but the sun was out, so he pulled a chair over and sat. Of course, before he even entertained the idea of taking the sheriff's job, he was going to have to consider Joey. What would he tell him about why he was wearing his daddy's badge?

And before he even thought about taking the job, he was going to have to go and talk to the mayor about this gang that only attacks towns during a holiday.

Chapter Twenty-Seven

When Clint got to City Hall Mrs. Babcock allowed him to go right in and see Mayor Edgewater.

"Well, this is a coincidence," the Mayor said. "I was going to come and see you. What brings you here?"

"To tell the truth, it was Mrs. Babcock. She came to see me this morning."

"Oh? I didn't ask her to do that."

"She told me it was her idea," Clint said. "In fact, she asked me not to tell you, but I thought you should know. She told me a wild story about you needing a lawman to keep your town from being attacked by a gang who only hits on holidays."

"Believe me," Mayor Edgewater said, "I know how that sounds, Mr. Adams, but it's true."

"You mean as far as you know, it's true," Clint said. "It seems to me no one has ever investigated these reports."

"I wanted Sheriff Owens to check them out, but he claimed each case was out of his jurisdiction."

"He was right," Clint said, "but he still could've gone and taken a look."

"I wish he'd felt that way," Edgewater said. "He and I really didn't see things the same way."

"Look," Clint said, "Mrs. Babcock seems to think I should wear the badge, but I just can't. I mean, I was pretty much with the man when he got killed. And I don't know how I'd explain wearing his badge to his wife and son."

"I understand."

"But still . . . this whole concept of a holiday gang is . . . is . . ."

"Unbelievable," the Mayor finished. "Well, the town council and I still got a couple of options."

"And look," Clint said, "I'm going to be around, possibly until Christmas. If anything happens, I'll be here."

"I'm just worried that the word will get out that we lost our lawman, and we'll go to the top of this gang's list," Edgewater said. "After all, we're the perfect, logical town for them to hit on Christmas."

"This gang—if it exists—isn't logical, at all," Clint said. "I'm sorry, but I can't pick up that badge."

Clint turned and left. Outside the mayor's office he stopped at Mrs. Babcock's desk.

"Did you do it?" she asked.

"I can't, Ma'am," he said. "I can't wear that badge, and the mayor understands. But I'll be around."

"I just hope that's good enough," she said.

***

After Clint Adams left, the Mayor turned and looked out the window at the street below. To him, Goodwill was the town that Christmas went to, to celebrate Christmas. To have it be looted, and possibly burned to the ground on that holiday was a heartbreaking thought.

If Clint Adams said he was going to be around until then, all the Mayor had to do was get the word out that the Gunsmith was in Goodwill. Then it wouldn't matter if they had a lawman or not. There would be easier pickings for the gang than a town where the Gunsmith was spending Christmas.

He turned when his office door opened again, and Mrs. Babcock came in.

"You're not angry with me, are you, Mr. Mayor?" she asked.

"No, I'm not," he said. "You thought you were doing the right thing."

"I don't understand why he won't wear the badge," she said.

"It's odd, but I do," he said. "And I have other ideas, so don't you worry about it. Just go back to your desk."

"Thank you, Mr. Mayor," she said, and withdrew.

He wanted to talk to the town council, but he wanted to do it individually, and not as part of a meeting.

He put on his hat and jacket and decided to get to it.

Chapter Twenty-Eight

Sheriff Owens had seemed to Clint to be a man who was very keen to do his job. It didn't make sense that he wouldn't go and check out at least one of the towns that the holiday gang had hit, just to make sure it had actually happened.

Christmas was under a week away. If this gang was going to hit Goodwill, Clint wanted to make sure Juliet and Joey were safe. He decided to go and see them and explain to Juliet that the mayor wanted him to pin on her husband's badge.

He figured she'd be in the store by now, having left Joey at school. As he walked into the mercantile, he saw her hand a brown paper wrapped package to a female customer and say, "Come again, Mrs. Henry, and Merry Christmas."

The older woman smiled, nodded and left.

When Juliet saw Clint, she stared at him but didn't say a word. At least, he thought, there wasn't a murderous glint in her eyes.

"What are you doin' here?" she asked.

"I wanted to talk to you," he said.

"About what?"

"Well, for one thing, your husband's badge."

"It isn't—wasn't—his. It belongs to the town."

"Well, the town has asked me to wear it," Clint said.

"And are you?"

"I don't want to," Clint said. "If I do, I'll have to explain it to Joey."

"You don't want the job?"

"No," he said, "I didn't come here looking for a job. I wore a badge years ago, and those days are behind me, but . . ."

"But what?"

Clint looked over at the door to the back room.

"Is Joey here, or in school?"

"He's in school," she said, then added, "if he'll stay there."

"Have you heard about a gang that attacks towns on holidays?"

"Oh, that?" she said. "Matt didn't believe that story and neither do I."

"Well, apparently, the mayor does," he said. "He thinks when word gets out that the sheriff is . . ."

"Dead," she said, "you can say it."

". . . dead, the gang will hit this town on Christmas Day."

"Really?" she said. "And you believe that?"

"I don't know what to believe," Clint said. "There's no proof that I can see one way or another."

"It's just a ridiculous idea," Juliet said. "Look, if you want to wear the badge, go ahead. It's not gonna bother me none."

"What about Joey?"

"He'll have to find out sooner or later."

"I was hoping later," Clint said, "but the word seems to be getting out, thanks to the undertaker."

"Then I suppose I better tell him," she said.

"How about if I tell him?" Clint suggested.

"Why?"

"I feel like I owe it to your husband," he explained. "I mean, he did ask my help in getting back here for Christmas. I should explain to Joey that I failed."

"No," she said, "don't tell him that. Tell him his father's dead, and how he died at the hands of the men he was hunting, but don't tell him you failed. He likes you too much. We can't take both men away from him."

"Very well," Clint said.

"Oh, and he wants you to come and help us decorate the tree," she said.

"Is that all right with you?"

"It's all right with me," she said. "for Joey's sake."

***

123

When the mayor returned to his office after he had been in private meetings with each of the town council members. It may have taken some talking, but they all eventually agreed with his plan.

"You've been gone all afternoon, Mr. Mayor," Mrs. Babcock observed.

"Was that a problem?" he asked her.

"No, no," she assured him, shaking her head, "there was no one looking for you. I was just getting ready to close the office."

"You can go on home, Mrs. Babcock," he said. "I'll lock up."

"Very well." She stood and put on her jacket. "Good-night, Mr. Mayor."

"Good-night."

She left and he went into his office. He poured himself a drink from a sidebar and carried it to his desk. If his plan worked, two things might happen. The town of Goodwill would definitely make it onto the map. Second, Clint Adams would probably be very angry.

If he was still alive when it was all over.

Chapter Twenty-Nine

Clint agreed to come to Juliet's house that night to help with the decorating.

"But as far as tellin' him his daddy's dead," she said, "let's see if we can put it off until after Christmas."

"Then we're going to have to keep him away from people," Clint said. "That means not sending him to school."

"That'll be easy," she said. "School's gonna be out until after New Year's."

"Okay, good," he said.

"Come by tonight at six," she said. "I'll feed you . . . again . . . and then we'll do the tree."

"I appreciate this, Juliet."

"Well," she said, "I thank you for being kind to Joey. But I'm still mad at you."

"Understood. I'll see you both tonight."

He left the store, feeling better about both Juliet and Joey.

***

At six o'clock Clint knocked on the door of Juliet's house. Joey answered the door and squealed, "It's Clint! Clint's here!"

"Well, let him in, child," Juliet said. "Supper's ready."

"Come on in, Clint," Joey said.

Clint entered then closed the door behind them.

"You boys wash up," Juliet said. "I'll put the food on the table."

While Clint and Joey washed, the boy said, "We're gonna decorate tonight."

"I know," Clint said. "I'm here to help."

"That's great!"

They dried their hands, went to the table and sat. Juliet laid out the food then sat with them. They all ate while Joey chattered away about how he wanted to decorate the tree.

". . . and Momma bought cotton so that the tree will look like it has snow on it."

"That'll be great," Clint said.

Juliet ate and listened but didn't smile. When they were finished, she cleared off the table, and brought out the decorations. There was garland, ribbons, cotton, and candles. There were also handmade cornucopias that would be filled with dried fruit, candy and nuts.

They let Joey start on the bottom branches, and then Clint lifted him so he could reach the middle and top ones. Juliet took care of the garland, while Clint held Joey so the boy could apply the cotton. After that, they filled the cornucopias and put them in place. The last thing to go on the tree were the candles, which Juliet placed. Then they all stood back to admire their work.

"Can we light the candles?" Joey asked.

"Not til Christmas Eve," his mother said. "It wouldn't be safe."

"Aw, Ma—" Joey started.

"Your Ma's right, Joey. It's dangerous, Joey," Clint said. "They could start a fire that would burn the house down. You wouldn't want that, would you?"

"No!" Joey said, his eyes wide.

"You can light them Christmas Eve like your mother said, and then keep an eye on them so there are no accidents. Does that sound okay?"

"Yes, sir."

"Good."

"Now go and get ready for bed, Joey," Juliet said, "and then come and say good-night to Clint."

"Yes, ma'am."

Joey left the room. Clint and Juliet stood back, looking at the tree from all angles. She stepped forward a couple of times to make a few adjustments, then seemed pleased.

"It's beautiful," she said. "We've never had such a large, beautiful tree."

"You both deserve it," he said.

"Well," she said, "Joey does."

Joey came running in, wearing his night shirt, and said "'night, Clint."

"Good-night, Joey."

"'night, Ma."

He kissed his mother and ran off to bed. Clint watched the boy go, experiencing feelings he wasn't used to.

"I guess I should get going," he said.

"You don't have to," she told him.

That surprised him. He thought she hated him for not telling her about her dead husband.

"I thought—" he started.

"I know what you thought," she said. "I was wrong to be angry. You were in a difficult situation and doing what you thought was right. You're good for Joey, Clint. I want you to be part of his Christmas—our Christmas. How about some coffee and pie?"

"Sounds great," he said, pleased that she had worked through her anger.

Chapter Thirty

If it was possible, the town became even more festive, the closer they got to Christmas Eve. The kids were
out of school and Clint spent as much time with Joey as
he could. He was intent on not letting the boy hear about
his father.

He also visited with the two saloon girls, Candy and
Velvet. As much as he would have liked to spend that
kind of time with Juliet, he did not approach her about it.
After all, she was newly widowed, and had a small son
and a reputation to consider.

He was sitting in the High Spade in the afternoon,
three days before Christmas. The girls were working the
floor and didn't have time for him just then. As the
holiday approached, the saloons became as busy during
the day as they were at night. That meant a lot of work
for the girls.

He was nursing a beer until it was time for him to go
to the store and pick up Joey for the afternoon, when
three men came through the batwing doors. They stopped
just inside and surveyed the room. He knew immediately
that they were gunhands. He didn't know if they were

looking for him or not, so he sat still and waited. Finally, they walked to the bar and ordered a bottle of whiskey.

Clint saw Candy and waved her over.

"You want another beer, lover?" she asked. "That's about all I can do for you right now."

"No," he said, "I mean, yes, I want another beer, but there is something else you can do for me."

"Name it," she said.

"Three men just came in. They're at the bar. One is tall with broad shoulders, the other two stand on either side of him because he's their boss."

"Yeah, I saw them when they came in," she said. "You can tell that from lookin' at them?"

"I can," he said.

"What do you want me to do?"

"Find out who they are, and why they're here."

"Should I just ask them?"

"No," he said. "Work your magic, and just see what you can hear, or what you can get them to say. Understand?"

"I get it," she said. "I'll do my best and come back with another beer for you."

"Good girl."

She flounced over to the bar where the three men were standing. She appeared to be talking to the bartender, but he knew she was listening. Then she spoke to one of the men, while the one in the middle—the boss—remained silent and ignored her. Finally, the boss leaned over and said something to her. She seemed to freeze, then turned and walked to Clint's table, carrying a beer.

"What happened?" he asked.

"The boss, he says he wants to talk to you."

"Did he mention me by name?"

"He did," she said, "and he has a . . . creepy voice. So raspy. Clint, I think the Devil has a voice like that."

"Ask him to come over here, Candy."

"A-all right."

She went back to the bar, spoke to the man and then got away from him as quickly as possible.

The man tossed off a shot glass of whiskey, asked the bartender for a beer, and carried it to Clint's table.

"Mind if I sit?" he asked. Clint heard what Candy meant about his voice.

"Why not?" Clint asked. "I assume you came in here looking for me."

"I did," the man admitted, sitting.

"What about your boys?"

"They're good where they are," he said.

"What's your name?" Clint asked.

"I'm Gabriel Dye," the man said. "You heard of me?"

"No, I can't say I have."

Dye seemed to be in his forties. When he took off his black hat and set it down on the table Clint could see his hair was black, shot through with grey in such a way as to make him seem to have horns. He wondered if this was deliberate. It also occurred to Clint, because of what Candy had said about the man, that Gabriel was the name of one of the seven fallen angels—who were led by Lucifer.

"And you're Clint Adams," Dye said. "I heard you were here." Dye frowned. "You're not wearin' a badge."

"Why would I be?"

"I heard this town lost its lawman," Dye said. "When I found out you were here, I assumed you were takin' his place."

"Again," Clint said, "why would I do that?"

"Maybe," Dye said, "to keep me and my gang from ridin' in here and burning this place to the ground."

Clint stared at the man.

"You haven't heard of me, but you've heard of my holiday gang," Dye said.

"I heard," Clint said, "but I didn't believe it."

"Oh, it's true."

"You ride into unprotected towns and loot and burn them?" Clint asked. "Why?"

"It's simple," Dye said. "Holidays lead to celebrations, and celebrations lead to carelessness. Understand? Easy pickin's."

Chapter Thirty-One

"There's got to be more to it than that," Clint said.

"Well," Dye said, "if you really want to nail it down, I like what I do."

"The looting, the burning . . ."

". . . the killin'," Dye finished. "Yeah, all of it."

"What kind of a childhood must you have had?" Clint asked.

Dye laughed.

"Can't blame it on my childhood," he said. "I was a happy kid. But when I got older, I found I liked hurtin' and killin' people. I also hate seein' people so happy on holidays—all holidays. Especially these end of the year ones, like Thanksgivin', Christmas and New Year's. What do people have to be so happy about?"

"But you only hit towns that don't have a lawman," Clint said. "Isn't that kind of cowardly?"

"No," Dye said, "it's smart. I mean, who'd ignore easy pickin's like that?"

"And your men?" Clint asked. "They go along with this?"

"Sure do."

"And what do you all do in between holidays?"

"Whatever we wanna do, as long as we come back together for the holiday. See?" Dye grinned. "We all celebrate in our own ways."

"This is sick," Clint said.

"That's what you say," Dye remarked. "To me it feels real natural."

Clint had known killers before, but he didn't think he'd ever known one like this.

"So if I put on the badge, you won't come here?" he asked.

Dye pointed a finger at him.

"I been thinkin' about that," he said. "Takin' down a town protected by the Gunsmith, now that would be memorable."

"So you're saying as long as I'm here, you're coming, badge or no badge?"

"I ain't gonna make it that easy on you, Adams," Dye said. "We're comin' in no matter what, whether you're here or not, whether you're wearin' a badge or not."

"So if they hire a sheriff other than me, you're still coming," Clint said.

"Yeah," Dye said, "that's what I'm sayin'. Look at this place. This is a plumb for us, Adams. This town celebrates Christmas like no other I've ever seen—so it's gotta pay."

Dye finished his beer and stood up.

"We'll be ridin' in here in three days," he said. "So get ready."

"And what if I don't let you walk out of this saloon?" Clint asked. "What if I kill you now?"

"Well, that'd be real interestin' to watch you try," Dye said. "Somebody in here might end up gettin' hurt."

Clint looked over at the bar, where the other two men stood with Candy between them, their hands on their guns, mean smiles on their faces.

"You get me?" Dye asked.

"I get you."

"I just thought I'd come to town, have a look at it, and meet you at the same time," Dye said. He touched the brim of his hat. "It's been a real pleasure."

Dye walked toward the batwing doors. His two men did the same, taking Candy with them. Then they walked out, leaving the frightened saloon girl standing in front of the swinging doors. Moments later, Clint could hear their horses. He stood up and walked over to Candy.

"You all right?"

"I'm fine," she said, "Those men, they're . . . evil. Especially the big one."

"That's exactly right," Clint said. "I don't know if I've ever met someone as evil."

"And at Christmas time," she added. "Are they gonna ruin Christmas for us?"

"Go back to work, Candy," he said. "You don't have to worry about it. Leave that to me."

"Okay, Clint."

She did as he said and melted back into the festive atmosphere of the saloon. Clint returned to his table and sat. The badge had absolutely nothing to do with it. The gang was coming in on Christmas Day, intent on burning Goodwill to the ground no matter what, whether Clint was there or not. If it wasn't for him, hiring a new lawman would have saved the town. Now, there was no stopping Gabriel Dye and his gang.

The whole thing still sounded ridiculous to Clint, but it was real.

***

Gabriel Dye and his two men reined in just outside of town. They turned and looked back at all the lights. When Dye saw that much celebration and happiness, it brought the taste of bile into his mouth.

"How'd it go, boss?" one man asked. "Adams gonna stay?"

"Oh, he'll stay," Dye said. "Boys, we got a date with the Gunsmith."

"Merry Christmas to us," the other man said, and they rode off, laughing.

Chapter Thirty-Two

The next morning Clint presented himself at the mayor's office early.

"Mr. Adams," Mrs. Babcock said, coldly. "What brings you here?"

"I need to speak with the mayor, Ma'am."

"I'm sorry, but he's very busy today," she said. "You'll have to make an appointment."

"This is serious, Mrs. Babcock," he said. "It has to do with the holiday attacks."

Her eyebrows went up.

"Have you changed your mind?"

"Not exactly."

She frowned.

"What does that mean?"

"It means that my mind might've been changed *for* me."

The frown deepened.

"I still don't understand," she said.

"The mayor can explain it to you," Clint said, "after I've explained it to him."

"Very well," she said, getting to her feet. "I'll tell him you're here."

She was back in moments, saying, "He'll see you now."

As Clint entered, the mayor remained behind his desk.

"Have a seat, Mr. Adams," Mayor Edgewater said. "Mrs. Babcock tells me you said this was serious."

"Yes." Clint sat. Edgewater did not offer him anything. "I had a visit last night from a man named Gabriel Dye."

"And am I supposed to know who that is?" Edgewater asked.

"No," Clint said, "but you will after Christmas."

"I don't under—oh, wait."

"That's right," Clint said. "He's the leader of this crazy holiday gang—and believe me, I do mean crazy."

The mayor looked shocked.

"He was here, in town?"

"Yes."

"Doing what?"

"Well, talking to me for one thing," Clint said, "but I suspect he was also looking the town over."

"Oh God."

"Exactly," Clint said. "Your town is in his crosshairs."

"Did he say when?"

"Yes, Christmas Day," Clint said. "He thinks it's only fitting."

"And what if we have a sheriff or marshal by then?" Edgewater asked. "I mean, I could put the badge on myself, if that's all it takes."

"It isn't."

"What do you mean?"

Clint related to the mayor his conversation with Gabriel Dye. The politician sat in rapt attention, his face growing redder and redder.

"He's crazy," he said, when Clint finished.

"I agree," Clint said. "He's stark raving mad. One of the saloon girls said he's evil."

"That sounds about right," the mayor said. "I assume you'll be leaving?"

"Why would I do that?"

"I thought, since you refused to wear our badge—have you changed your mind?"

"Not about wearing the badge," Clint said, "but I guess I'm going to have to do something about this gang."

"Will you hunt them?"

"No," Clint said, "I don't have any idea how many there are. It wouldn't be smart for me to go hunting them alone."

"Then what do you intend to do?"

"This town is going to have to make a stand, Mr. Mayor," Clint said.

"How can we do that?" Edgewater asked. "This is a town of storekeepers and civilians. We have no gunmen, and I don't know of anyone here who has even served in the military."

"Then that leaves me three days to do some training, doesn't it?" Clint asked.

"They're coming on Christmas Day?" Edgewater asked.

"That's the whole point for them," Clint said, "to do it on the holiday."

"We're supposed to have a huge celebration that day," the mayor said.

"Before you can do that," Clint said, "you're going to have to make sure you have a town."

"Jesus," Edgewater said, "that's what lawmen are for."

"Even if you had a sheriff," Clint said, "he couldn't do it alone. This town is going to have to defend itself."

"If I tell everyone now that the gang is coming in three days, many of them will take that time to pack and leave."

"That's between you and your citizens, Mr. Mayor," Clint said. "If you want to get out and leave everything to this gang, it's up to you."

"We have a lot invested in this town," Edgewater complained. "We can't just up and leave."

"Then you better call a meeting so I can talk to your citizens," Clint said. "We have to get started now!"

Chapter Thirty-Three

The decorations in the room belied the seriousness of the meeting that was about to take place. Most of the people present had no idea what lay ahead and were still smiling and wishing each a happy holiday season.

Clint stood at the front of the room with the mayor, while the members of the town council simply sat with the rest of the citizens.

"All right, let's settle down," the mayor called out, waving his hands. "Take your seats or stand in the back. We have to get this underway."

People stopped exchanging good wishes and found their places.

"First of all, some of you may not know that Sheriff Owens has been killed."

"That's the worst kept secret in town!" somebody yelled.

"Well, his son doesn't know it yet," the mayor said, "and we'd like to keep it that way."

"Don't the boy deserve to know his daddy's dead?" somebody else asked.

"He does," the mayor said, "but that can wait til after Christmas, can't it?"

People began to nod their agreement.

"All right, but that isn't the main reason we're here," the mayor said. "I'm sure some of you have heard the stories about this gang that attacks towns on holidays."

"That ain't a real thing!" a man's voice called out and laughed.

"Oh, I'm afraid it is," the mayor said, "and they attack towns they know don't have a lawman."

"You sayin' they're comin' here?" somebody asked.

"That's what I'm saying," the mayor said, "on Christmas Day."

That brought angry responses from the crowd, and then somebody shouted, "So name a lawman!"

"I'd love to," the mayor said. "Anybody here volunteer?"

Nobody responded.

"I didn't think so," the mayor said. "We have a man here who thinks he has a solution. This is Clint Adams. I think we should listen to what he has to say."

"Wait a minute!" somebody shouted. "That's the Gunsmith. Let him stand up to this gang."

"Alone?" the mayor asked.

"He's the Gunsmith," another voice yelled.

"First of all," the mayor said, "he doesn't live here, he's only visiting. What makes you think he'd stand alone against a gang for us?"

"Let's hear what he has to say," a woman called out.

Everyone fell quiet, then, and Clint realized that it was Juliet who had spoken from the back. He wondered where Joey was if she was here?

"I met the leader of this gang," Clint said. "He's crazy. He says they're coming in Christmas Day, no matter what. Whether I'm here or not, whether there's a lawman or not."

"But why?" somebody asked.

"For one thing," Clint said, "he's crazy, like I said. For another, he hates all this fuss you make over Christmas."

"Then let's take down the decorations," somebody suggested.

"That won't change anything," Clint said. "They're coming."

"Then we have to get out," somebody yelled.

"I ain't leavin' my home," another said. "Besides, three days ain't enough time to get packed up."

"It is for me," a third voice said. "I'll just take my family and git!"

"And go where?" the mayor asked.

"Anywhere!"

"Those of you who want to leave," Clint said, "I won't try to talk you out of it. But those of you who want to stay because it's your home, I'll tell you what we have to do. Make up your minds. If you're leaving, leave now."

Several people stood immediately and left. Others moved hesitantly, starting to stand, then sitting, then standing again and looking around. Finally, all those who were going to leave had done so, and about two-thirds were left.

"All right," Clint said, "those of you who are staying, you're going to have to fight."

"We ain't fighters," a man called out, "we're store-keepers."

Juliet stood up.

"The store I work in isn't mine, but I'll fight for it, and for my home."

"She's the sheriff's widow, of course she wants to fight," somebody said.

"This gang had nothing to do with killing the sheriff," Clint pointed out.

"I'm just going to defend my home," Juliet said. "It's got nothing to do with my husband. And I trust Mr. Adams."

A man stood up.

"Are you sayin' we gotta fight, and you're gonna fight with us?" he asked.

"I'm going to fight with you," Clint said, "and tell you how we're going to do it. Are you all willing to listen?"

Apparently, they were.

Chapter Thirty-Four

Clint outlined the plan he had come up with.

"How do we get started?" a man called out.

"Who can shoot?" Clint said. "I don't need to know that you've never shot anyone. If you've hunted, you can shoot. When we're done here, I'd like you to stay if you have a gun and can shoot."

"Men and women?" a woman's voice called out.

"Unfortunately, yes," Clint said. "We'll need all the guns we can get."

"All right then, that's it," the mayor said. "Like Mr. Adams said, stay behind if you can shoot. The rest of you . . . go home."

People began to file out. Clint was pleased to see that about half the population had stayed—mostly men. There were only a few women present, including Juliet. There was no way he was going to put Juliet in the line of fire, but he wasn't about to tell her that now.

He counted the people in the room. There were more than twenty. From experience he would have figured four or five of them could actually shoot. He was going to have to use the others just to make noise. They needed to sound like they had a good size force.

"If you'll line up single file here, I'd like to find out what kind of gun you have, and what your experience is. That way I'll know where to place you."

He spent the next hour speaking to each person and making notes. He made sure he memorized the names of the four or five he thought could actually shoot.

"Mayor, I need an open area somewhere, maybe an empty lot so I can see how these people shoot."

"There's an open part of Tremont Street you can use," Edgewater told him.

"Good," Clint said, "I'll need somebody to collect cans and bottles we can shoot at."

"I'll have it done," the mayor promised. "In an hour?"

"That's good."

All of the people in the room agreed to meet Clint at that location in an hour. After everyone left—including the mayor—Clint held Juliet back.

"You're not fighting," he told her.

Her face grew red.

"Why not?"

"Joey's why not," Clint said. "He's already lost one parent. I'm not going to be the reason he loses both."

"Stop bein' so full of yourself. You wouldn't be the reason," she told him. "It would be that crazy man you're talkin' about."

"That may be," Clint said, "but you're going to stay home with Joey."

"And what do I do if that gang manages to burn down the town?"

"Your house is on the edge of town," Clint said. "You and Joey will be safe there. Whatever happens, I'll come and get you."

"I can shoot, Clint."

"Good," he said. "You'll stay in your house with your rifle in your hands. It's going to be your job to make sure Joey is safe."

She shook her head.

"This is not the Christmas I had planned for him."

"If we can stave off this gang," Clint said, "this town will still have its Christmas."

"And if we can't?"

"Then it's going to be a sad holiday," he admitted.

***

Clint was waiting at the empty lot where people began to arrive with their guns. Some had pistols, other had rifles.

He lined them all up single file and had them shoot, one at a time. After most of them missed their targets, he selected the three most experienced hunters and had them work with five people each, on aiming and firing and, hopefully, hitting what they shot at.

The mayor wasn't there when they started, but he came along sometime later. He watched a few minutes, then moved up alongside Clint.

"This doesn't look good," he said.

"You should have been here an hour ago."

"Is this going to work, Clint?" Edgewater asked. "Or are we fooling ourselves?"

"We're doing what we can, Mr. Mayor," Clint said. "We can't just curl up and hope they don't come."

"I know that."

"I've got three men here who are experienced hunters. They can shoot. That's a start."

"Can you do something in three days?"

"I have to," Clint said. "There's no other choice."

Edgewater didn't reply.

"Is there?" Clint asked.

Edgewater scowled, said, "No," and walked away.

Chapter Thirty-Five

Clint worked all afternoon and only lost a few, who simply could not hit what they aimed at, or got too exhausted to continue. In the end, he ended up with a dozen guns, nine men, and three women.

"Let's take a walk through town," he said to them. "I want to see where we can put you."

Clint decided the rooftops and second floor windows were the best. By putting his guns up high like that, it wouldn't really matter which direction the gang came in from. Also, by placing some of them on the roofs, those people would be able to see the gang ahead of time, as it approached town, and offer a warning.

"There, there and there," Clint said, pointing. He put men on the rooftops, and ladies in the windows. "Here's the important part. Even if you see that you're not hitting anybody with your shots, keep firing. We need the noise. It has to sound like we have a solid force."

As dusk approached, he finally told the people they were done for the day.

"Head home, and after supper, clean your weapons," Clint said. "We have to make sure they work properly when the time comes."

The dozen nodded, but Clint saw two men in the back with their heads together.

"All right, this is important," he yelled. "If you think you're not going to be there when I need you, let me know. Don't just stay home on Christmas Day. If you're not going to come, I need to have time to change plans."

They all nodded and agreed. Clint was sure he was going to lose some to overwhelming fear when the day came, but he thought he'd be able to count on at least ten.

As they scattered and returned to their homes, Clint realized he had no idea how large Dye's gang was. They could've been ten or a hundred, or something in between. If there was a telegraph office in town, he might have been able to find out, but as it was, he was going to have to operate blind. They wouldn't know how large the gang was until they showed up.

He realized he was hungry and decided to simply eat at his hotel.

***

About twenty miles north of Goodwill was a small town called Spartansville. Sitting in the only saloon in town was Gabriel Dye's gang, while Dye was upstairs with a young lady.

"Why is it?" Denny Graves said, "that the smaller the town, the longer its name?"

Hank Lane stared at him from across the table and asked, "Why do you even think of questions like that?"

Graves shrugged.

"Seems to me we sit around and do nothin' a lot," he said. "Makes me think, is all."

"Well then, think to yerself," Lane said. "Don't ask them stupid questions out loud."

"If you don't like my questions," Graves said, "why don't you sit someplace else?"

"No problem," Lane said, getting up and moving away.

The saloon was small, and most of the gang was inside. There really weren't too many other places to go, so Lane went to the bar.

"Whatsamatta?" a man known only as Musto asked. He was tall and thin, about ten years older than most of the other men, with a black patch over his left eye. At forty-five, he'd been riding with Gabriel Dye the longest.

"Ah," Lane said, "Danny keeps askin' them stupid questions of his."

"He ain't got nothin' better to do," Musto said. "Ignore him."

J.R. Roberts

"I wish I could." He waved at the bartender for another beer. "Musto, whataya think of hittin' this town with the Gunsmith in it?"

"Now who's askin' stupid questions, kid," Musto said. Lane was in his late twenties, the youngest of Gabriel Dye's twenty men. "Dye tells us what towns we're hittin' and we hit 'em. It don't matter who's there."

"Yeah, but the Gunsmith—"

"Even the Gunsmith can't stand against twenty men, Lane," Musto said. "And Dye warned 'im. If he's a smart man, he'll get the hell outta that town before we get there."

"Goodwill sure is a pretty town, though," Lane said. "Too bad we gotta do it."

"You know Dye don't like pretty towns, kid," Musto said.

Lane accepted his fresh beer from the bartender and sipped it.

"You know," he said, "when I was just a boy, we celebrated Christmas—"

"Kid," Musto said, "you better stop right there. Drink your beer and don't let Dye hear you talkin' about Christmas. You got it?"

"I got it, Musto, I got it."

156

Chapter Thirty-Six

Gabriel Dye flipped the woman over onto her belly and smacked her generous butt cheeks. There were other, younger whores in town, but he wanted this one. She was older, experienced, and she still had a good body on her, especially her bottom.

"Get up on your knees," he told her.

"Are you sure about this?" she asked.

"Don't worry," he said. "It ain't gonna hurt."

"The men I've been with just wanna rut and rut and then go to sleep. None of them ever flip me over."

"Believe, me, darlin'," he said, "you look great from this angle."

"You know, a whore my age has usually done everythin', but I ain't never done this."

"There's a first time for everythin'," he said.

"But . . . you're so big," she said, making her tone sound as little girl as possible, "are you sure you're gonna fit?"

"Don't worry, sweetie," he said, getting on his knees behind her. "I'll fit." He took hold of her hips. "Are you ready?"

He couldn't see her face, so she rolled her eyes and said, "I'm ready, but be gentle. Like I toldja, this is my first time."

"Oh yeah," he said, spreading her ass cheeks so he could see her little brown bum hole, "I'll be real gentle."

He pressed the head of his large cock against that hole, and pushed . . .

***

Later, Dye pulled his trousers on while the woman rubbed her butt with both hands.

"So?" he asked. "Not so bad, huh? I learned that from a French whore in New Orleans."

"It was just fine, Gabriel," she said.

"Next time I'm gonna show you somethin' else I learned in New Orleans."

"From another French whore?"

"No," he said, "this one was a Cajun whore."

"You sure been with a lot of whores, Gabriel," she said.

"All I got time for is whores, darlin'," he said.

"And you got the money for them, too, right, honey?" she asked.

He laughed, took some money out of his trousers pocket and set it on the dresser.

"There ya go, Ava," he said, "and you earned it."

"Come back any time, big boy," she said, and added to herself, any time you've got the money, otherwise stay the hell away.

"I'm just gonna get myself somethin' to eat," he said. "I'll be back later."

As he went out the door she called out, "Can't wait, lover!"

***

His men saw Dye coming down the stairs. They all had orders from Musto not to talk to Gabriel Dye, unless he spoke to them first.

Dye walked across the saloon floor to the bar, and by the time he got there, Musto had a cold beer waiting for him.

"Thanks, Must," he said. He drank half of it down right away, then wiped his mouth with the back of his hand. "That Ava, she knows how to give a man a ride. You ougtta go up there, Must."

"That's okay, Gabe," Musto said. "I get my women when I need them."

"Yeah, I seen the women you get, Musto" Dye said. "Young and skinny. What kinda ride can you get from some skinny little whore?"

159

"It all depends on what you like," Musto said.

Dye looked around the small saloon.

"How're the boys doin'?" he asked. "Are they all ready for Goodwill?"

"They're ready," Musto said.

"They know about the Gunsmith?"

"I told 'em."

"And?"

"They're ready," Musto said. "In fact, they're more than ready."

"Christmas Day," Dye said. "Not before. They know the rules."

"Yeah, they do," Musto said.

Dye signaled the bartender for two more beers.

"Drink that down and we'll go get somethin' to eat," he told Musto. "I have a whore waitin' for me upstairs, and I ain't as young as I used ta be."

"None of us is," Musto said.

Chapter Thirty-Seven

Two days before Christmas, Clint had his shooters out in the field, firing at bottles and cans. Later, he took them to their rooftop and second-floor positions, so they would all know where they should be, come Christmas Day.

Meanwhile, the town continued to plan for their holiday festivities. The mayor was doing his best to convince everyone that things would go as planned.

Clint allowed his shooters to go home for supper with their families. He had his own supper, and then went to the High Spade Saloon.

"Where've you been?" Candy asked, coming up to him.

"Busy," he said.

"We heard," she said. "You're gonna save the town."

"You left out the word 'try,'" he said.

"I have faith in you," she said, patting him on the chest. "Many of us do."

She went off into the busy atmosphere of the saloon, and he went to the crowded bar. He managed to clear a space for himself and wave to the bartender.

"Beer," he said.

"Comin' up."

The man brought the beer over and set it down.

"Thanks."

"On the house," the bartender said.

"Why's that?"

"You're the man who's gonna save Christmas," the bartender said.

"Who told you that?"

"Everybody in town knows it."

"I'm not going to be able to do it alone," Clint pointed out.

"Well, we hear you've got yourself a small army."

"Not exactly," Clint said. "I've got some people who supposedly can shoot."

"And you tellin' them how and when," the barman said. "That's all we need."

"The only question is, what kind of Christmas Day is it going to be?"

"It's gonna be the same kind we always have," the bartender said. "That is, after all the ruckus is over."

As the bartender moved down the bar to serve other customers, Clint wondered just how many people were thinking the same way the barman and Velvet were.

He decided to find out what two people in particular were thinking.

***

Juliet opened the door in response to his knock and smiled.

"Look who's here," she said. "Come on in. Joey will be glad to see you."

"Thanks."

He entered and was surprised. The house was much more decorated than the last time he was there. There was fruit, flowers, garland, strung up popcorn, and the candles on the tree were burning.

"Clint!" Joey shouted. "Merry Christmas."

"Merry Christmas, Joey," Clint said, catching the boy as he threw his little body at him. "It looks like you've been real busy."

"Me and Ma did it," Joey said. "We want Santa Claus to be real happy when he gets here."

"I think he will be," Clint said.

"You should've come for supper," Juliet told him.

"He can come tomorrow night, can't he, Ma?" Joey asked. "For Christmas Eve supper?"

"I think Clint's going to be pretty busy, Joey," Juliet said.

"I think I can make it," Clint said. "I mean, if that's an invitation."

"Of course it is," Juliet said. "We'll be glad to have you."

"Joey, I'll see you tomorrow night."

"Yaaaaay!" Joey said. "Tomorrow night you can help me put the angel at the top of the tree."

"I'll be happy to help," Clint said.

"Joey, get ready for bed," Juliet said. "Thank you for agreein' to come by tomorrow night," she said to Clint. "It'll mean a lot to Joey."

"I'm happy to do it."

"But . . . what brought you by tonight?"

"I was just checking . . . I've been hearing that . . . well, I'm the savior of the town."

"That's what I've been hearin'," she said. "Are you surprised?"

"To tell the truth, yes." he said.

"I thought maybe it was you who was spreadin' the word," she said.

"Why would I do that?"

"I thought you were trying to make the whole town believe everythin' was gonna be all right." She studied his face then asked timidly, "everythin' is gonna be all right, isn't it, Clint?"

"I'm going to do my best, Juliet," Clint said, "but only time will tell. Let's just make Christmas Eve very special for Joey, no matter what."

"Agreed," she said, putting her hand on his arm. "Thank you."

"I'll see you tomorrow night," he said. "Can I bring anything?"

"Just your appetite," she said. "Oh, and your strong arms, to hold Joey up so he can put the angel on the top of the tree. His father was supposed to do it, but every year . . . well, at least this year Joey's not expectin' him."

"Did you tell him—"

"No, no, I haven't told him yet that his father's dead," she said. "But he just doesn't expect him to be back for Christmas. And that's all right, because he's very happy you're here."

"He's a fine boy, Juliet," Clint said. "You're doing a great job raising him."

"I just hope I can keep it up," she said.

Chapter Thirty-Eight

Clint went back to the High Spade Saloon. The next day was Christmas Eve, and he was going to have to spend most of it getting his people into place. On Christmas morning, they'd have to be on their rooftops and in their windows with guns, ready and waiting.

It remained to be seen if the town would be alive on that day, or if people would stay behind locked doors, waiting for the outcome. While training his people Clint had seen many loaded wagons leaving town, as some of the citizens took their families and belongings and ran. On some streets he saw boarded up doors and windows that people were planning to hide behind.

One way or another, he was going to have to kill Gabriel Dye. Once that man was gone, the holiday gang would disband, for it was Dye whose hatred fueled their deadly campaigns.

Clint would need his highly untrained force to keep the gang busy while he concentrated on Dye. If he could kill him early in the exchange, the fight would be over before it started.

He was finishing his beer when Velvet sidled up to him.

"You look . . . lost," she said.

"Not lost," he said, "just . . . concerned."

"With Christmas Day?"

"Yes."

"Don't be."

"Why not?"

She put her hand on his arm.

"You're gonna save this town," she said.

"I wish people would stop saying that," he said. "I'm not a savior."

"You know what you need tonight?" Velvet asked.

"What?"

"A distraction . . . or two."

"What are you proposing?"

"A distraction," she said, pointing to herself, then, "or two," pointing at Candy.

"When?"

"We're finished here, at one," she said.

"I'll be here at five minutes to," he said.

She smiled and said, "Perfect."

As she melted back into the activity of the saloon, he thought she was probably right. A distraction for tonight was just what he needed. And he already knew from experience that Velvet and Candy were very distracting.

***

Clint went back to his room at the Yuletide Hotel, tried to read, then started thinking about Christmas Day. He had his people in place. But now, in his head, he began moving them around. Normally, when he was facing a confrontation like this, he had guns he could rely on to watch his back. But in this instance, he was pretty much on his own. None of these people had any experience, and they were going to be too busy watching their own backs.

Before he knew it, it was time to go back to the High Spade for his "distractions."

***

"The girls are upstairs," the barman said. "They said you should go on up."

"I'll have a beer first," Clint said.

"Sure."

The bartender set the cold beer in front of him and said, "On the house."

Clint didn't argue. He took the beer and headed for the stairs.

Chapter Thirty-Nine

When he knocked on the door, one of the girls sang out, "Come on in."

He opened it, thinking he probably should have brought a bottle of champagne with him, rather than just a beer for himself. But the first thing he saw on the table in the corner of the room was a bucket with a bottle in it.

"Hello, Clint," Candy said, from the bed.

Both girls were in the bed, with the sheet pulled up to their necks. Velvet was holding a glass of champagne.

"Welcome," she said, raising the glass.

"Ladies," he said, "thank you for the invitation."

"Well," Candy said, "we figure you have a lot on your mind."

"You need to relax for a while," Velvet said. "And we doubt you'll have any time for it, starting tomorrow morning."

"You're absolutely right," he said.

"So," Candy said, tossing the sheet back, "we're ready for you.

"Now you need to get ready for us," Velvet said.

Both girls were stark naked under the sheet and ready, indeed. He could smell their sexual arousal from across the room, as well as feel the combined heat of their bodies.

"Then I guess I better get to it," he said. He walked to the table holding the champagne bottle and set his beer down next to it. He started to undress, gunbelt first, then sat on one of the chairs to remove his boots. His clothes followed very quickly, and by the time he was naked, he was also very ready. Both girls stared at his hard, jutting cock with hungry eyes.

"Bring that over here," Velvet said.

He walked to the bed and they both moved to the edge to run their hands over him. Candy fondled his cock-and-balls while Velvet stroked his thighs and buttocks. While they did that, he reached down to run his hands over their smooth skin.

Eventually, they took hold of him and pulled him onto the bed. He reclined on his back while they nestled down between his thighs together. They ran their mouths over his inner thighs, biting, kissing, and moving on to his penis and testicles. They each ran their tongue up one side of his hard cock, their mouths meeting at the top. They kissed each other, then took turns taking him into their mouths and sucking him. When they got him to the point where he didn't think he could take anymore, he changed position. He got them onto their backs, lying side-by-side, and went down between their thighs. He used his mouth first on Candy, at the same time using his fingers on Velvet. He managed to take them to the heights of their pleasure so that they gushed and moaned at the same time. Then he switched, getting between Velvet's generous thighs, using his mouth on her delectable vagina, while using his fingers on Candy's. This time Velvet managed to finish first, her juices soaking his mouth and chin, and then moments later Candy wet his fingers, and hand, and the bed beneath her thoroughly.

He got to his knees then and took turns fucking them, first Candy, then Velvet, then back to Candy. Velvet had the body type he preferred for sex, cushy and padded, but Candy reacted differently, made different sounds while she writhed beneath him. The noises she made inflamed him even more, but he was able to keep going as they each cried out when their time came, again and again. Finally, he couldn't hold back any longer, and erupted inside of Velvet while Candy got to her knees behind him, ran her hands over his back and buttocks, kissing his neck and shoulders while he emptied into her friend . . .

***

"Jesus," Velvet said, a few minutes later. "I was wonderin' which one of us you were gonna finish in."

"Did you know?" Candy asked. "Did you know which one?"

"No," he said, "I didn't. It was just time."

They were all lying on their backs, naked, with Clint between them. Both girls had a hand on him, stroking his thigh leisurely. At the same time, he ran a hand over each of them.

"Which one of us do you like the best?" Velvet asked.

"Now is that a question you really think I'm going to answer?" he asked.

Candy giggled.

"I told you, Velvet," she said, "I told you he wouldn't say."

"Do you girls always do this together?" he asked.

"No," Candy said, "when we have sex for business, we do it separately. But with you it's for pleasure."

"We thought it would be fun being with you like this," Velvet said, "and we were right."

"Yes," he said, "you were right. It has been fun."

"Is it over?" Candy asked.

"For now," he said. He slid down to the bottom of the bed and got to his feet. "I have to get back to my room. I need to go over my strategy for Christmas Day."

"But tomorrow's Christmas Eve," Velvet said. "Do you know what you'll be doing tomorrow night?"

"Yes," he said, starting to dress while they watched. "I'm hoping to make a young boy's Christmas Eve memorable."

Chapter Forty

He woke the next morning, knowing that this was going to be the hardest Christmas he had ever had. But spending the holiday with Juliet and Joey, might be the best he had ever had.

After breakfast, he decided he could not arrive at Juliet's house empty handed. He needed to buy gifts for her and Joey, but she worked at the mercantile store. He needed to see if she was there and try to do some shopping when she wasn't.

The first time he went to check it at about nine a.m., there was a young man working behind the counter. He entered the store and looked around. Just to make sure Juliet wasn't there, then approached the man.

"Merry Christmas! Can I help ya with somethin', sir?" he asked, with a smile.

"Do you have any idea when Juliet will be coming to work?" Clint asked.

"Oh, she has the next few days off, sir," the young man said. "In fact, I think we all have tomorrow off."

"Because it's Christmas Day?" Clint asked.

"Well," the young man said, "I don't know if you heard, but there's supposed to be a gang comin' to town to, uh, I don't know, rob us? Ruin Christmas?"

"That sounds terrible."

"I know," the lad said. "Some folks have even left town."

"Why are you still here?" Clint asked.

"I heard the Gunsmith's in town, and he's gonna save us," the boy said. "I gotta tell ya, that's somethin' I wanna see."

"And what if he doesn't save you?" Clint asked.

"Um, well, they say he's gonna do it," the young man said, "and he's the Gunsmith."

"So you just assume he's going to save the town?"

"Well, yessir," the clerk said, "otherwise I guess we're all gonna be . . . in trouble."

"Well," Clint said, "I guess I better get my Christmas shopping done."

"What're ya lookin' for, sir?"

"I need presents for a lady," Clint said, "and for a small boy."

"I think we can get ya both," the clerk said. "Lemme show you some lady's stuff, first. Right back here . . .

***

Clint spent an hour in the store, and, while he was there, no other customers came in. The streets had been pretty deserted when he walked over. He wondered if the citizens were already locking themselves in their homes, just in case the gang came a day early.

He was hoping to meet his people at noon and go over the plan one last time. He also figured that would be the time he would discover just how many of them would actually show up on Christmas morning.

He thanked the young man for his help and carried the gifts back to his hotel room. At eleven-thirty he left and went to meet his people at the empty lot.

***

There were eight men and two women now. The women were in their forties and had each spent much time hunting to feed their kids. But their kids were grown now, their husbands were gone—one was widowed, and one had been abandoned—and they felt as if they had nothing to lose by putting themselves at risk to save the town.

The men were all in their thirties and forties. He didn't want any younger or older, so he had rejected several others who wanted to volunteer. The younger ones would be too impulsive, and the older too stubborn in their ways.

He had them all stand in a line and then, one-by-one, he checked their weapons to see if they were clean and in proper working order. He told at least half of them to clean the weapons again that night, more thoroughly.

Three of the men were very experienced hunters. Their guns were in perfect working order, and Clint felt he could make the most use of them.

Four of them only had pistols. On the first day he told them each to get a rifle. They were now among those who had to clean them, again. He had them fire and fire until they were feeling more comfortable.

"Why can't we use our pistols?" one had asked.

"Because," Clint said, "you're not going to get close enough. If this works, we won't have to engage these men at close quarters."

By the time he finished explaining his strategy, he had them all nodding their heads in understanding.

"All right," he said, "let's take a walk and see where our positions will be."

They walked through the empty streets to the center of town, where Clint determined they should engage the gang.

"You there, you there, you there, and you there," he said, pointing.

"And us?" one of the women asked.

"Come with me, ladies, and I'll show you."

"What about us?" a man asked.

"I want the four of you down here, on the ground," Clint said. "Two of you find cover on that side of the street, and two on the other side."

"Gotcha, boss."

"Ladies," Clint said, "shall we?"

Chapter Forty-One

When Clint had his people in place, he went back down to the street, stood in the center and looked around. The streets were still pretty empty of bystanders, and the few that were out seemed to be scurrying to their destinations.

Admittedly, Clint could have used some people more experienced with gun play, or simply more people with guns. Considering the gang would have to ride in and be vulnerable for a finite period of time, the more lead that was rained down on them, the better.

He looked around at the decorations, which were probably going to inflame Gabriel Dye's insane hatred of Christmas even more as he rode in. But the mayor and the town fathers would not entertain the thought of taking the decorations down.

"We're depending on you to save us, Mr. Adams," Mayor Edgewater had said, the last time they spoke. "Removing our decorations would be giving in to them."

He brought his people back down to the street.

"I want you all down here at first light tomorrow," Clint said. "You have to tell me now if you're not going to come."

They all exchanged glances, but nobody spoke up.

"Dexter," he said, pointing to one man, "I want you out here at five a.m., before first light. Get up on your rooftop and keep watch. The minute you see anything— riders, or the dust cloud a gang of riders would kick up— I want to hear about it. Got it?"

"Got it," Dexter said. He was one of the three men Clint was going to rely on most.

"All right, then," Clint said. "Go spend Christmas Eve with your families."

They disbanded and went their separate ways, wishing Clint and one another a Merry Christmas.

Rather than go back to his hotel just yet, Clint walked over to the High Spade which, at midday Christmas Eve, was not doing a brisk business.

"Is this how it always is on Christmas Eve?" Clint asked.

"Not at all," the bartender said. "We usually get busy early on this day, but I think somethin' might be brewin' that's changin' that this year, don't you?"

"Speaking of brewing," Clint said, "let me have a beer."

"Comin' up."

When the bartender returned with the beer Clint asked, "Where are the girls today?"

"Still sleepin'," the barman said. "Somethin' musta wore 'em out yesterday."

Clint ignored that comment just as he ignored the one about trouble brewing.

"So how's it goin'?" the bartender asked. "Setting up our defenses, I mean."

"I could use more guns," Clint admitted.

"Hey, I'd get out there, but I'd only shoot somebody on our side by accident."

"When the gang gets here, I'd just like to show them a lot bodies carrying iron," Clint said.

"You think that'd change their minds and they'd leave?" the barman asked.

"No," Clint said. "Their leader's too crazy. He'd come in alone, if he had to."

"If he did that, you'd be able to handle him alone," the man said.

"Probably," Clint said, "but it's not going to happen that way."

The batwing doors opened, and Mayor Edgewater walked in.

"Mr. Mayor," Clint said. "Join me for a beer."

"I was just walking around town," Edgewater said, as the bartender set a beer in front of him. "Christmas Eve is never this dead."

"Well, the word has certainly gotten around," Clint said. "The gang's coming in tomorrow, but folks are afraid to take any chances. They don't want to get caught in the street."

"Tell me the truth," Edgewater said, "are you going to be able to fight them off?"

"I'll tell you the God's honest truth, Mayor," Clint said. "We're going to put up a fight."

The mayor waited for more, and when it was not forthcoming he said, "That's it?"

"That's all I can promise you."

"Adams," the mayor said, "there are folks here who didn't leave town because you said you were going to save them."

"I don't think I ever said that," Clint said. "All I did was ask for volunteers to put up a fight."

"I don't think folks are going to remember it that way," the mayor said.

"Well, I can't help what people thought they heard, Mr. Mayor," Clint said.

"Jesus," Edgewater said, and downed his beer. "Jesus," he said again, breathlessly.

"You could always grab a gun and get out there with us, Mr. Mayor," Clint said.

Edgewater approached like he was considering the request, then looked at the bartender and said, "Give me another beer."

Chapter Forty-Two

Clint would have stayed the afternoon in the nearly empty saloon, but he didn't want to smell like beer when he went to spend Christmas Eve with Juliet and Joey. So, he went to his room and busied himself wrapping the gifts he had bought for them. He then tried to do some reading. But he couldn't clear his mind of what was going to happen the next day.

When it was time to leave and head for Juliet's, he realized that his arms would be full if he walked there. If any of Gabriel Dye's men were in town and they caught him that way, he'd be a dead man. The same was true if he tried to ride there on the Tobiano. He decided to go to the livery and rent a buggy.

The hostler was glad to accommodate him and didn't charge him for the horse and buggy.

"After all," the man said, "it's Christmas, and you're savin' our town."

"If I was you," Clint said, "I'd stay off the street to-morrow, unless you have a gun."

"Huh, not me," he said. "I do all my work with horses, not guns. By the way, that Tobiano is in fine fettle."

"Good," Clint said. "Keep him that way."

"I'll hitch up that horse for ya."

***

Clint got the gifts loaded into the buggy and drove it to Juliet's house. He knocked on the door and it was swung open by Joey.

"Clint's here!" He threw his arms around Clint's waist.

"Merry Christmas, Joey."

Joey didn't seem to notice the buggy, which suited Clint. He wanted to get the gifts under the tree after the boy went to bed that night. He stepped into the house with Joey still attached to his waist and closed the door behind them.

"Merry Christmas," Juliet said. "Supper will be ready in an hour."

"We have to put the angel on top of the tree, Clint!" Joey said, excitedly.

"Let's get to it, then," Clint said.

"I'll get the angel," Joey said, and ran from the room.

"He keeps it under his bed," she said. "I had it made even before he was born, and he loves it."

Joey came running back, carrying the porcelain angel.

"See this hole?" he said, holding it so Clint could see the bottom. "It will fit right over the top branch." He ran to the tree. "Lift me up, lift me up!"

Clint walked to the tree, picked Joey up and held him over his head. The boy reached out with the angel and slid it over the top branch.

"I got it! I got it!"

Instead of lowering the boy, Clint shifted so that he was holding Joey straight over his head, flat out as if he was flying.

"Wheeee!" the boy shouted, while Clint ran around the room with him. "I'm flyin', Ma, I'm flyin'."

"Take it easy, you two," Juliet shouted, laughing.

"Okay, that's it," Clint said, bringing the boy down and putting him on his feet.

"Wow, that was great!" Joey shouted. "And look." He pointed to the top of the tree. "Ain't she pretty?"

"She's very pretty, Joey," Clint said, but he was looking at Juliet, not at the angel. It made her blush.

"I've got to get my cornbread in the oven," she said.

"I'll help."

"Joey, go and play in your room until supper's ready."

"Okay, Ma."

"I'm glad you sent him away,' Clint said. "I've got a buggy outside with presents for the tree. We can put them under there when he goes to bed."

"You didn't have to do that, Clint."

"Sure I did," Clint said. "It's Christmas Eve. And we don't know what's going to happen tomorrow."

She turned to face him.

"I've been thinking about that," she said. "Why don't you, and I and Joey pack up and leave tomorrow? Instead of you waiting for the gang to ride into town."

"I can't do that, Juliet," he said, "but you can. I've got that buggy outside. You and Joey can get on it and ride out. Get away from this town before the fighting starts."

"Where would we go?"

"Go to Buckley," Clint said. "Wait there until you hear from me."

"And if we don't hear from you?"

"Then things probably didn't go well," he said. "You and Joey will have to settle somewhere else. Someplace where you won't have to deal with this crazy gang."

"Let's not talk about it, anymore," she said. "Let's just enjoy Christmas Eve."

"I have a book in the buggy, too," Clint said. "I thought I'd read it to Joey."

"What book?"

"Dickens' A Christmas Carol," Clint said.

"That has ghosts in it, doesn't it?"

"Well, yeah, but—"

"I wouldn't want to read him anything that might scare him," she said. "I have something else you can read."

"It's the poem 'A Visit from St. Nicholas.' Some people call it 'The Night Before Christmas.'"

"I know it," Clint said. "I'll be happy to read it to him."

"Good," she said.

Chapter Forty-Three

Juliet's Christmas Eve supper was a feast. Joey could barely chew because of the smile that was on his face the whole time. The boy was having a great Christmas Eve, which was what his mother and Clint both wanted.

After supper, Juliet cut up a special cake she had made for Christmas. She and Clint each had a slice with coffee, while Joey had two slices with milk.

"That was yummy," the boy said, wiping his milk mustache on his arm. "Can I have another one, Ma?"

"No, Joey," she said, "two is enough. I don't want you going to bed with a tummy ache."

"Will you put a piece out for St. Nick so he can have it when he comes with my presents?"

"You know I will," she said. "Now let's go and sit on the sofa and Clint is gonna read to us."

"Oh boy!" Joey said, running to the sofa. "Whataya gonna read, Clint?"

"It's a Christmas poem, Joey," Clint said, picking up the book Juliet had given him.

Juliet sat next to Joey, who snuggled up against her, while Clint sat in a chair across from them.

"It's called 'A Visit from St. Nicholas,'" Clint said, and started reading. "Twas the night before Christmas, and all through the house . . ."

***

Gabriel Dye gave Ava the whore a proper poke, then made her suck him until he was hard again. This time he put her on her back and pounded away at her until he exploded yet again. Then he rolled onto his back to catch his breath.

Ava snuggled up to him and put her head on his shoulder, knowing he liked that. She tried to give him everything he liked, because then he was generous.

"This is some Christmas Eve," she said, drawing designs on his hairy chest with her forefinger. "I'm gettin' all my presents early."

"You ain't gettin' any presents," he said.

He pushed her hand away from his chest.

"Do you wanna get paid tonight?"

"Okay, okay," she said, rolling onto her back, "you hate Christmas."

"You bet I do," Dye said. "I hate all holidays. What a waste. And tomorrow one town is going to pay for all that waste."

"What town is that?" she asked. Then her eyes went wide. "Not this one! This is where I live. You ain't gonna—"

"No, no," he said, annoyed, "not this town, a town called Goodwill."

"Oh," she said, "the Christmas town."

"Is that what you call it?"

"That's what everybody around here calls it," she said. "They go all out and light the place up with decorations."

"Well, I'm gonna light it up, too," he said, "with fire."

"Jesus," she said, "what about the people?"

"That's up to them," he said. "Now, you see that hard thing between my legs?"

"See it?" she asked. "I been feelin' it front and back all night."

"Well now I want you to get down there and suck it for all you're worth," he said. "You make me a happy man, and I'll be real generous."

"Whatever you say, daddy," she said, sliding down between his legs.

"And If you don't make me happy," he said, "daddy's gonna be real mad. You understand?"

"I understand," she said, and started licking the length of his hard cock.

***

Joey was asleep before Clint could finish reading the poem.

"I'll take him," he told Juliet. He put the book aside, rose and picked the boy up in his arms. As he carried him to bed Joey asked, without opening his eyes, "Clint, is Santa gonna come?"

"You bet he's going to come, Joey," Clint said. "But you have to be fast asleep."

"G'night, Clint."

"Good-night, little guy."

By the time he set Joey down on his bed, the boy was fast asleep, again.

Clint came out and found Juliet still sitting on the sofa, crying softly. He sat down next to her and took her into his arms.

"Take it easy," he said. "It'll all be over tomorrow, one way or another."

"Joey and I are gonna wait right here, Clint," she said. "I don't wanna take him away from his home."

"Like I said," he replied, "your house is far enough away that the gang will miss it. Even if they burn down the whole town."

"Oh, God," she said, "I don't understand why everyone in town hasn't just left."

"The same reason you're not leaving," he said. "It's their home."

"And they trust you to save it," she said.

"I told them I'd do my best," he said, "but they're not stepping up to help."

"I thought you had help."

"I've got ten people to help me and most of them can't shoot," Clint said. "I'm going to do my best, but I didn't promise anyone I'd save the town. That's not a promise I would make."

"It's your reputation," she said. "It's a way people have faith in you, and maybe it'll have an effect on the other side, too."

"These are hardened gang members, Juliet," he said. "My name alone is not going to change their minds."

"Then I suppose your gun will have to do that, Clint" she said.

"I'm sure going to try my best to make that true," he told her.

Chapter Forty-Four

Once Juliet had cried herself out, they continued to sit on the sofa, side-by-side.

"Has Joey mentioned his dad?" Clint asked.

"Not at all," she said. "I think he's just happy that we—he—has you with us—him—this year."

"And do you miss his dad?"

"Sadly, no," she said. "We weren't gettin' along at all, and I think we were on the verge of splittin' up. We just didn't know how to tell Joey."

"So I guess that's why he wanted to make sure he got back here in time for Christmas," Clint said. "Because it might be his last one with his son."

"The day after Christmas I'll have to tell Joey his dad is dead," Juliet said, "so we can bury him. I just hope he's not gonna be buried along with the whole town."

"Look," Clint said, "if things work out the way I've planned—"

"Stop," she said.

"Why?"

"The only thing I want," she said, "is for Joey and me, and you, to be safe and sound the day after Christmas. Whatever else happens . . . happens." She shrugged.

"I can't commit myself to this task with that attitude," Clint said. "Whatever happens will hopefully be what I make happen." He stood up from the sofa. "I better go back to my hotel and get some rest."

"You know," she said, taking his hand, "you could spend the night here."

"I don't think that would be a good idea, Juliet," Clint said. "I wouldn't want to have to try to explain that to Joey. He still thinks his dad is out there."

She released his hand.

"You're right, of course."

"Not that I wouldn't want to," he told her.

He took her hand this time, pulled her to her feet and kissed her. Then they both looked at the door to the bedroom to be sure Joey wasn't standing there.

"Let's get those gifts from the buggy and put them under the tree," he said, "and then I'll go back to town."

They went out together and collected the packages, brought them in and placed them beneath the tree. She stopped with one in her hand.

"This one has my name on it," she said.

"There might be one or two more like that there," he admitted.

"You didn't have to do that, Clint."

"Well, we couldn't have Joey opening presents on Christmas morning with none there for you."

When they finished, they stood back and admired their work. The tree, as festive as it was, looked even moreso with gifts beneath it, even though most of them were simply wrapped in brown paper.

She walked him to the door then.

"Is there any chance you might be here when Joey opens his gifts?"

"I suppose that will depend on when the gang decides to ride in," he told her.

"Of course."

"You just remember," he said, "no matter what you see or hear, stay home and don't come to town."

"Of course."

"And keep your rifle handy," he said. "Just in case."

She hugged herself, as if she felt a chill.

"Suddenly I'm wondering if I should've taken Joey away from here," she said.

"You could do that in the morning," he suggested, "if you still feel that way when you wake up. Just make sure you head away from town."

"Right."

He kissed her again and said, "With any luck, I'll see you for Christmas supper."

"Oh, good," she kidded, "you want me to cook again?"

Chapter Forty-Five

Clint woke before first light. He wanted to make sure his man Dexter was on his rooftop at five a.m. It was the roof of a two-story hotel called The Gold Leaf, and, when Clint got there, Dexter was waiting out front.

"Good man," Clint said. "Now get up there and keep a sharp eye out."

"You got it, boss."

"Sound the alarm if you see anything," Clint said.

"And how do I do that?" Dexter asked.

"Yell, fire a shot, do whatever you have to do to get everyone's attention."

"Right."

Dexter went into the hotel. Clint looked up and down the street, didn't see any of his other people yet. He wondered what he would do if they didn't show up. Face the gang alone? He had no way of knowing how many there would be. Five he could handle with some degree of confidence, but more than that would be a problem.

He was still wondering when he saw two people approaching, a man and a woman, each carrying rifles. They were both bundled up against the cold with jackets and scarfs.

"We thought we'd come early," the man said.

"Have you had breakfast?" Clint asked.

"I'm too nervous to eat," the woman said.

"Believe me," Clint said, "this would be better done on a full stomach. Your name is Mrs. Adcock?"

"Just call me Lizzie," she said. "Everybody in town does."

"Lizzie, would you be insulted if I asked you to go get some sandwiches so we can all eat right here?"

"Son, when you get to be my age nothin' offends you, anymore." He had originally thought she was in her forties, but now he was thinking fifties.

"Egg sandwiches okay?" she asked.

"That'd be perfect. Here." He gave her some money. "There should be eleven of us here, so get a couple of dozen sandwiches."

"What do I do about coffee? Bring an urn?"

He laughed.

"We'll have to make do with water," he said. "A few canteens should do it."

"I can get that, too," she said. "I'll be right back."

Clint turned toward the man.

"Are you her husband?" he asked.

"What? Lizzie and me? Not a chance."

"What's your name, then?"

"Tallman, Herb Tallman."

"Okay, Herb," Clint said, "I want you on that roof-top. That's a hardware store. Do you know the people who own it?"

"I do."

"See if they'll let you in so you can get to the roof," Clint said.

The man was the opposite of Lizzie. While he looked like he could be sixty, he was probably fifty.

"What about my sandwich?"

"I'll have it brought up to you."

"Thanks."

Tallman crossed the street to the hardware store.

As first light began to break, Clint saw four more of his people approaching on the empty street, three men and the other woman.

"This is strange," one of the men said. "This street is never empty on Christmas morning."

"I'm sure there's never been this threat before," Clint said. "Have you had breakfast?"

"Just coffee," one said, and the others nodded.

"I think we're all too nervous to eat," the woman said.

"Well, Lizzie's coming back with egg sandwiches for everyone," Clint said. "I want you all to eat at least one. We don't know how long we'll be out here waiting. Take up your positions and I'll have Lizzie bring them to you."

They all nodded and headed for their positions.

He was expecting the last three of his group, and hoped they'd show up soon.

***

Gabriel Dye was on his horse at first light, waiting. Eventually, his men started to assemble around him.

The first was Musto.

"Where are they?" Dye asked.

"They're comin', boss," Musto said. "Believe me, they're all lookin' forward to goin' up against the Gunsmith."

"Yeah, as a group," Dye said. "As if twenty men would get a reputation for killin' the Gunsmith."

"That's true," Musto said. "None of them want to face him alone."

Hank Lane came riding up next, quickly followed by the other men.

"It's about fuckin' time!" Dye shouted.

"You said first light, boss," Lane said.

"Yeah, yeah," Dye said. He looked at Musto. "Let's get 'em goin'."

"Right, boss." Musto looked at Lane. "Come on."

"What's eatin' him?" Lane asked.

"He's anxious to get this done," Musto said. "He takes the fact that the town of Goodwill exists as an insult."

"Jesus," Lane said, "he's crazy. He really hates holidays that much?"

"Especially Christmas," Musto said. "And if you hafta ask me that, whataya been doin' here all this time?"

"I do it for the money," Lane said. "That's what the rest of us do it for. I think most of the men actually like Christmas."

"Well, just don't let Dye hear you say that," Musto advised.

They reached the assemblage of men who were waiting on horseback.

"Listen up," Musto said. "Nobody rides into Goodwill until Dye says so. Nobody fires a gun until Dye says so. And nobody starts a fire until he says so. Got it?"

The men all nodded their heads.

"We got it, Musto," Lane said. "Same as always. Dye calls the play."

"That's right," Musto said. "I'm gonna ride up ahead with Dye, you lead the men."

"And take a head count," Musto said. "If we don't have twenty, somebody's gonna be sorry."

"Um," Lane said, "is that twenty plus you, me, and Dye, or twenty altogether?"

Musto rode on ahead without answering.

Chapter Forty-Six

Dexter ate his sandwich and kept his eyes peeled on the horizon. He also turned and looked in the other directions, in case the gang decided to come in on some other road besides the main one. Clint Adams seemed to think they were just going to ride straight down the main street.

Speaking of which, he moved to the edge of the roof and looked down at the street. At that moment Clint Adams looked up and Dexter signaled all clear. Clint waved his thanks.

Dexter went back to staring off at the horizon, where the Gunsmith expected the gang to appear.

***

Clint was almost dead sure the gang would be coming at the town head on. After all, their arrival was not unexpected. There would be no reason to try to sneak in—and a gang couldn't sneak in.

He considered putting some of his people on horseback outside of town, to be on the lookout in all directions, but there was a possibility they might get caught out there, and he needed all their guns to be in the same place at the same time.

Quite a few of them were concerned with the fact that they had never fired at a person before. They thought they might be nervous and miss. He told them all the same thing.

"This gang is coming right at us," he said. "They'll be coming down that street clustered together. It'll be impossible to miss."

It almost sounded ludicrous, but from Clint's one meeting with Gabriel Dye, he thought the man had a pretty big ego. Dye assumed his gang was just going to ride in and take Goodwill apart. Clint hoped he was going to be very surprised.

Everybody had eaten their food, so they all had full bellies. Clint knew that people usually felt better once they had been fed, even if they didn't think they were hungry to begin with.

Clint still wasn't sure what his own position would be. He would have liked to just stand in the middle of the street, but that would depend on how many were in the gang. But he knew he would be on the ground. He just didn't know where. He was hoping Gabriel Dye would lead his gang into town. All he needed was one clear shot. Once Dye was dead, the rest of the gang would be easier to handle. It was Dye's hatred that was directing them. Without him they would probably lose focus.

He hoped.

***

Joey woke his mother by yelling, "It's Christmas!"

"So it is," she said, yawning. The look of glee on his face made her momentarily forget the bad news she had to tell her little boy.

"Can we open presents?" he asked.

"Of course we can," she said, "but I have to make breakfast, honey."

"Is Clint comin' for breakfast?" the boy asked, anxiously. "Is he gonna watch me open my presents?"

"No," she told him, "but he said he'd be here later on."

"He will," Joey said, "if he said he'll be here, he will. He's not like Pa. He keeps *his* promises."

"He'll try, Joey," she told him. She couldn't tell him Clint would only come if he was alive, just as she couldn't quite tell him his Pa was dead. She was amazed they had been able to keep that from him for this long. Once he went to town, or back to school, he was sure to hear the news, so she had to tell him before that.

But first . . . Christmas.

Chapter Forty-Seven

As the gang approached the town of Goodwill, Gabriel Dye held his hand up to stop their progress.

"Lane!"

Lane rode up alongside his boss.

"Ride up ahead and tell me what you see."

"Right boss."

Dye dismounted as Lane urged his horse into a trot. Musto also stepped down. The others remained mounted.

"What are you expectin' to see?" Musto asked.

"The Gunsmith, for one," Dye said, "but I'm sure he's managed to dredge up some help. I'd like to know just how much."

"Does it matter?" Musto asked. "We're gonna ride in there and wipe the town out. It don't matter who's standin' in our way."

"We're talkin' about the Gunsmith, Musto," Dye said. "He's got somethin' up his sleeve."

"The way I figure it," Musto said. "he'll be lookin' to kill you as soon as he can. I know you like to lead us in these raids, but I think this time you better bring up the rear. Or better yet, stay right in the center of the pack. Let us protect you on all sides."

"You have a point," Dye said. "Let's see what Lane has to say when he gets back."

It wasn't long before Lane came riding back.

"The street looks empty," he said, "but there was a man up on a rooftop."

"Keepin' an eye out for us, no doubt," Dye said. "Adams must have his other men hidden."

"You think he's got shooters?" Lane asked.

"I think he's got men with rifles," Dye said. "Whether or not they can hit anythin' is the question."

"They're probably mostly townspeople," Musto said. "Shopkeepers, not shooters."

"Still," Dye said, "they'll be slingin' lead. I think I'll take your suggestion, Musto."

"Come on," Musto said, "let's build you a pocket of protection."

They rode back to the rest of the men.

***

Clint saw Dexter waving at him from the roof. He crossed the street to be closer.

"What is it?"

"One man," Dexter said. "Seemed like he took a look at the town and then rode away."

"Dye sent a man up ahead," Clint said. "I'm sure all he saw was you. Keep a sharp eye out, Dexter. I think they're almost here."

"Right."

Clint went to all the other positions and told his people to get ready.

"We been ready!" Lizzie called back.

Clint had the feeling she was going to be one of his best fighters.

***

With Dye riding mid-pack, Musto took to the front of the column and led the gang toward Goodwill. There were a few of the gang members who didn't like the idea of Dye "hiding" among them, but they didn't speak up. Most of the others didn't care, they were just looking forward to dealing with the Gunsmith, and then taking the town apart. They didn't particularly care where Dye was riding.

***

"Here they come!" Dexter shouted. There was just a tinge of panic in his voice, which he fought to control.

"How many?" Clint asked.

"Must be twenty, maybe more," Dexter said.

Two-to-one odds, Clint thought. It could've been worse.

Clint decided to wait right in the center of the street for them. That brazen a move might throw them off. He had his rifle in his left hand, and his right hand down by his side.

"Get ready!" he called out. "You start firing when I do."

***

Lane came riding up alongside Musto.

"You really think we should just go ridin' in like this?" he asked.

"It's what we always do," Musto said.

"I know, but this is a little different," Lane said. "We're dealin' with the Gunsmith."

"He's just a man," Musto said, "standin' against twenty."

"But if he's got help—"

"Shopkeepers," Musto said, "not the Earp Brothers and Doc Holliday."

"Yeah, but Musto—"

"Fall back, Lane," Musto said. "We're almost there."

Chapter Forty-Eight

The sounds of the horse's hooves pounding announced the arrival of the gang.

As the riders came into view, Clint looked for Gabriel Dye, but didn't see him. He had expected the man to be right up front, and had planned to fire at him first, try to get the attack over with quickly. Dye had either sent the gang in ahead of him, or he wasn't coming. The latter seemed unlikely, since this was his attack.

Clint stood his ground as the gang approached, and abruptly the man leading them raised his hand to call them to a stop.

"I'll bet you're Clint Adams," he said.

"That's right. And who are you?"

"Musto," the man said, "just call me Musto."

Musto appeared tall and lean as he sat his horse with ease. He had a gun on his left hip, and Clint could tell he knew how to use it.

"Where's Dye?" Clint asked.

"He's here," Musto said. "Do you intend to stand in our way, Mr. Adams?"

"I do."

"You'll stand against more than twenty of us?"

"I have some help."

Clint raised his arm and his force of ten appeared on rooftops, and in windows, pointing their rifles.

Musto looked around at the gun barrels, and then back at Clint.

"Doesn't look like enough," he said.

"We'll make do," Clint said. "Now why don't you tell your boss to come out of hiding? I assume he's in there among the men?"

"You'd like a clean shot at him, wouldn't you?" Musto asked.

"No," Clint said, "I'd *love* a clean shot."

Musto looked around at the rifle barrels again, then he raised his own hand and Clint heard the metallic clicks of rifles and pistols.

"Any way I can talk you out of trying to destroy this town?" Clint asked. "I mean, look at it. Have you ever seen a place decorated so beautifully?"

"Exactly why we're gonna destroy it," Musto said.

"Get to it, then," Clint said.

Musto raised his hand and then dropped it. Clint saw the man and the riders behind him tense to start their horses forward. He drew his gun and started firing, at the same time running from the center of the street.

The rifles on the rooftops and in the windows began to bark . . .

***

Gabriel Dye heard the lead striking flesh around him, as his men struggled to return fire. He didn't know why they were struggling. If they stayed calm, they would have been able to pick out their targets all around them.

He sensed that the deadly fire was coming from the ground, probably from the guns of the Gunsmith. He realized he had made a mistake, allowing Musto to convince him to stay covered up. If he had been out in front of his men, he could have taken care of Clint Adams straight away.

He drew his gun and returned fire. His aim was deadly. He dispatched one man from a roof, and another from a window. His closest count told him there were about eight more.

A few of the gang members had been shot off their horses. The loose animals were rearing in panic, and more than one of them slammed into Dye's horse, throwing his aim off. He knew he had to get out into the open to be more effective.

***

Musto and Lane were firing calm and accurately, but the rest of the gang were rushing their shots and panicking as some of their numbers hit the ground. They weren't used to getting this much resistance. Usually they rode into one of these towns and simply took it over.

The flying lead began to shred some of the decorations on either side of the street. Musto realized what was happening and turned to his men.

"Take cover!" he shouted and leaped from his own horse.

Following his example, the gang members began to drop off their horses to scamper out of the street, seeking cover.

"Jesus," Musto said, as he saw Clint Adams step away from cover with his gun in his hand. The Gunsmith began to deal out death with every shot.

***

Clint had hustled out of the street and into a doorway, from where he fired, reloaded, and fired, the result of which was gang members being shot from their saddles. He also noticed that a few of the shots coming from rooftops and windows were hitting home with enough frequency that the gang was affected.

Clint saw Musto drop from his saddle and shout or-ders. As the rest of the gang followed, he stepped out from cover and began to fire with even more accuracy. Then he saw Gabriel Dye, still on his horse. The gang leader was firing high, at Clint's people, and was doing damage. This was Clint's cleanest chance at Dye, and he was going to take it. But as he turned to fire, both Musto and Lane fired at him. Their bullets whizzed past his head, and he was forced to duck. He fired at Dye, but a loose horse slammed into Dye, almost knocking him and his horse down, causing Clint's shot to miss.

Holstering his empty pistol Clint raised his rifle and fired slowly and deliberately . . .

***

Musto saw Adams step from cover. He and Lane immediately fired at him, but both missed. Adams quickly raised his rifle and fired, striking Lane in the belly. Musto ducked for cover as Adams continued to fire calmly, killing two more gang members.

Things were not going the way they usually did. This gang was so used to working unopposed that they were not reacting well.

Feet on the ground, Musto looked around and spotted Gabriel Dye, still mounted, firing his gun as quickly as he could. Then, suddenly, Dye turned his horse and started riding out of town.

He was running . . .

***

Dye saw things going wrong and couldn't accept the blame for it. Instead, he blamed his gang for reacting badly to the resistance they had encountered.

He saw Musto and Lane firing back, then saw Lane fold in half and slump to the ground. Musto kept firing.

He also saw Clint Adams, standing out in the open, firing like a madman. And lead kept raining down from above, most of it an annoyance, but some of it hitting home.

He looked around at the number of his men lying on the ground, and knew it was over. He looked over at Musto, still firing. He was going to have to leave him on his own.

He yanked on his reins, turned his horse, and started riding out of town.

***

Clint's first instinct was to jump on a horse and chase Gabriel Dye. But, on second thought, he didn't want to leave his people. There were still enough gang members to make a battle. If he left, his people might fall apart. So he stayed, and kept firing.

The man called Musto was firing his weapon and shouting orders. With Dye gone, he was obviously the leader. Clint was going to have to stick to his plan but change his target from Dye to Musto.

Riderless horses were milling about on the street, and Clint used them to work his way across. When he finally stepped away from a horse, he found himself facing Musto, who didn't look surprised.

"Looks like your boss lit out," Clint said.

"Obviously," Musto said.

They were each holding their gun.

"We could try shooting each other," Clint said, "or you could call off what's left of your men."

Shots were still being fired around them.

"And you'll do the same?" Musto asked.

"Yes."

"Then what?"

"To tell you the truth, I don't know," Clint said. "There's no law here. So I just might let you go. It's Dye I want."

Musto stared at Clint, then tossed his gun to the ground.

"Stop firing!" he shouted. "Stop!"

"Hold your fire!" Clint shouted to his people.

It suddenly became quiet.

"You know," Musto said, "Dye's just gonna put together another gang so he can continue his crazy attacks. He'll be back here next year."

"No, he won't," Clint said, "because I'm going to catch him."

Chapter Forty-Nine

The mayor opened the sheriff's office so Clint could put Musto and the remainder of the gang in cells. Twenty-three men had attacked Goodwill, eight ended up in cells.

"We killed fifteen of 'em?" Lizzie asked.

"I think we killed three," Dexter said. "One got away. Mr. Adams killed the rest."

"So," Lizzie said, refusing to have her pride dashed, "we killed three of 'em."

Clint came out of the cell block.

"We also lost two of ours," he told her. He looked around the room at the others. "The eight of you did well. You can go home to your families, and your Christmas now. You saved your town."

As the eight of them filed out, Musto shouted from the cell block, "Hey, Adams!"

Clint went back into the block. There were only two cells, and he had put four men in each.

"I've got two injured men here," Musto said.

"I'll have the doc come over and have a look. Anything else?"

"Somethin' to eat."

"I'll see about it."

"And," Musto continued, "you said you were gonna let us go."

"I said *maybe*," Clint said, and left the cell block.

He looked around the small office. Since his arrival, he hadn't spent any time there. He didn't see the need. He wasn't the sheriff. And he still wasn't.

The door opened and the mayor walked in.

"Is it over?" he asked.

"Not quite."

"What do you mean?"

"I have to go out and track down Gabriel Dye," Clint said. "Then it'll be over."

"Why not let him go?" Edgewater asked.

"Because if we do, he'll just put together another gang. He'll train them better this time. And they'll come back next year."

"Jesus."

"You're going to need a judge, and you'll have to put a badge on somebody. Even if it's temporary, but you'll need somebody here while you have prisoners."

"Can you suggest anyone?"

"Yes," Clint said, "A woman named Lizzie, or a man named Dexter."

"If I give Lizzie a badge, she'll be insufferable," Mayor Edgewater said. "I'll pin it on Dexter until we can find a permanent sheriff to replace Owens."

"Good. And now your town can enjoy their Christmas today. Tell the people they can go back to the streets. They'll probably want to replace the decorations we shot up this morning."

Clint headed for the door.

"Are you going after this fella Dye, now?" the mayor asked.

"I can't let him get too far ahead of me, Mayor."

"But . . . it's Christmas."

"And it almost wasn't, thanks to him. I'm not going to leave him to do this to some other town. Or to come back next year, because I won't be here then."

"Next year we'll have a lawman," Edgewater said. "He doesn't attack towns that have lawmen."

"Believe me, Mr. Mayor," Clint said, "after what happened today, he'll make an exception."

"But—" Edgewater started, but Clint was out the door and gone, heading for the livery stable.

When he got to the stable, he found the hostler holding the Tobiano's reins, having already saddled him.

"When I heard the commotion, I thought you might be needin' him," the man said.

"Good thinking," Clint said. "Thanks."

"Thank you for savin' Christmas, Mr. Adams."

"I had help," Clint said. "And now I'm going to finish the job."

Chapter Fifty

Clint made one stop before lighting out after Gabriel Dye. He rode to Juliet's house, hoping he would get to her without seeing Joey. As it turned out, she was looking out the window since hearing the shots. When she saw him, she came outside.

"Is it over?" she asked. "Are you all right?"

"I'm fine," Clint said, "but it's not over. Dye escaped."

"And the town?"

"It's safe."

"Then why isn't it over?"

"Because I can't let him go," he said, and gave her the same reasoning he had given the mayor.

"But . . . why you?" she asked. "You're not the sheriff."

"I started this, Juliet," he said, "I have to finish it. Where's Joey?"

"He's inside, by the Christmas tree. He wanted you to be here when he opened his presents."

"I know," Clint said. "I wanted to be."

"I told him to start and he opened a few," she said.

"Well," he said, "go in and—"

"Clint!" Joey yelled, coming out the door. "You're here. I knew you'd be here."

Clint dismounted and walked over to Joey, got down on one knee in front of him.

"I can't stay, Joey."

"Why not?"

"Because a bad man escaped, and I have to go and catch him."

"But you ain't the sheriff!"

"I know, but I have to do it."

Joey frowned mightily.

"Then you're just like my Pa," he complained. "You said you'd be here for Christmas, but you're not."

"Well," Clint said, "if I can catch him quickly, I'll be back tonight, for Christmas supper. Meanwhile, you open all your presents that St. Nick brought you."

"I will," Joey snapped. "I was waitin' for you, but now I'm gonna open 'em all!" He turned and ran back into the house.

"I'll talk to him," she promised. "He'll forgive you. And I suppose I'd better tell him about his father."

"Can I do that?" Clint asked. "Let him open his gifts, and I'll tell him tonight."

"All right," she said. "But you better come back safely."

"I'll be back," Clint promised, "and I'll be bringing with me the man who started this all."

Chapter Fifty-One

Clint started on the street where the firefight had taken place. Snow on the ground had fallen several days before. The gang had churned it up as they approached town. He would have to get far enough away from the trail left by the entire gang. He needed to find tracks left by a single horse—Gabriel Dye's.

But he needed a clue.

He rode to the jailhouse and entered, found Dexter sitting behind the desk, fingering the badge on his chest.

"Hello, Sheriff."

"Mr. Adams," Dexter said, dropping his hand from the badge. "I understand I have you to thank for this."

"It's just temporary, Dexter," Clint said. "That is, unless you really want the job. That'll be between you and the mayor. Meanwhile, I need to see the prisoners."

"Sure, go ahead," Dexter said. "You want the key?"

"No," Clint said, "I don't need to open a cell."

Clint went into the block, stood in front of the cell being shared by Musto and three of his men.

"Adams," Musto said, coming to the front of the cell, "you said you'd let us go."

"That's going to be up to a judge, Musto," Clint said. "But if you were to help me, I could make a recommendation."

"Help you . . . how?" Musto asked, squinting suspiciously.

"Where was Dye headed when he lit out from here?" Clint asked.

"How the hell would I know?" Musto demanded.

"You must have some idea where he'd go for help, or shelter," Clint said.

"You mean like friends?" Musto laughed. "Dye's got no friends, Adams."

"A woman, then," Clint said. "He must have a woman tucked away somewhere."

Musto opened his mouth to answer, then stopped himself.

"There *is* a whore he likes," the man admitted. "Her name's Ava. She's in Spartansville."

"And where is Spartansville?" Clint asked.

"About twenty miles north of here."

"You think he's going there?"

"Let's put it this way," Musto said. "I don't know where else he might go."

"You mean to tell me you and Dye never went anywhere together?"

"That's right," Musto said. "We all meet in Spartansville before each holiday. That is, the ones who want to be in on his next raid."

"So it's not always the same gang?"

"No," Musto said, "it's usually Dye, me and whoever shows up."

"So how long would it take Dye to put together another gang?"

"Without me?" Musto asked. "A long time."

"So if I let you out, Musto," Clint asked, "would you join up with him again?"

"This might keep me in this cell a little longer," Musto admitted, "but probably."

"Then I'll have to bring him in before I can let you go," Clint said.

"That makes sense," Musto said. "So if I was you, Adams, I'd head for Spartansville."

"If you were me," Clint said.

"Yep."

"Are you sending me into a trap?"

"Nope."

"How can I be sure?"

"You can't," Musto said, "but I don't wanna be in here any longer than I have to, so take my advice, or leave it."

"I guess," Clint said, "I'm going to have to take it."

227

He left the cell block.

"I heard all that," Dexter said. "You want me to come with you?"

"No, Dexter," Clint said, "the mayor wants you here. I'll be back, with Gabriel Dye."

"And what if you have to kill him?" Dexter asked.

"Then I'll be back with his body," Clint said. "But one way or another, this whole holiday gang thing ends now."

"I wish you luck."

"Thanks."

As Clint left the sheriff's office and started for his horse, he saw the mayor approaching.

"Are you heading out?" Mayor Edgewater asked.

"I am," Clint said. "Dye might be in Spartansville. I'm going there to check. If he's not, there's a woman there who might be able to tell me where he is."

"Adams, I want all these men in the cells to be hanged."

"That won't be up to you, Mr. Mayor, it'll be up to a judge."

"Well, I'll make sure there's a judge here within two days. I'm sending a man to Deadwood, where there's a telegraph."

"Two days?"

"That's right."

"I'm hoping to be back tonight," Clint said, "but who knows? I should certainly be back in two days."

"Do you object to hanging these men?" Edgewater asked. "After all, they killed two of our citizens."

"If it's what a judge wants to do, I have no objection," Clint said. After all, he never did promise Musto he would let him go. Just that he'd speak for him if his information led him to Dye.

"The one we want to hang is Gabriel Dye, though," Clint said.

"Well, bring him back," Edgewater said, "and we'll string him up with the others."

Clint looked around. There were people on the street again, smiling, wishing each other Merry Christmas, repairing decorations. A mass hanging sure as hell wouldn't be in the Christmas spirit, but the mayor seemed adamant about it.

He was going to ask who the judge was but stopped himself. No matter what name the mayor would have said, he wouldn't have known him.

"I better get going," Clint sad. "If Dye's in Spartansville, I'll be back tonight."

"Then I hope he is," Edgewater said. "And I don't particularly care if you bring him back dead or alive."

"I'll keep that in mind," Clint said, mounted up and riding out.

229

Chapter Fifty-Two

Spartansville was a long name for a small town.

As Clint rode in, he saw one hotel, one saloon, a trading post, no sheriff's office and no City Hall. No wonder Dye liked to gather his men here.

There were tracks heading in and out of town. From the number of them Clint assumed they had been left by the gang. There was no way to pick one out that was recent.

Clint reined in the Tobiano in front of the saloon, tied him off and entered. There were a few customers on this Christmas Day, but Clint doubted this was different from any other day. Not in this town. He approached the bar and slapped his palm on it to arouse the dozing bartender.

"Wha—oh, can I help ya?"

"I'm looking for Gabriel Dye," Clint said.

The bartender stiffened and said, "Who?"

"Come on," Clint said, "you know who I mean. The man who comes here with his gang."

"G-gang?"

Clint took his gun out and placed it on the bar. It wasn't something he liked doing, but he was looking for a shortcut here.

The customers looked up from their tables, saw the gun, and stood up to leave.

"Everybody sit down!" Clint yelled.

There were three of them, each at their own table. They sat. But while they were standing, Clint noticed two of them were wearing sidearms.

"Nobody leaves," Clint said. "I'm looking for Gabriel Dye. Where is he?"

Nobody answered.

"You," Clint said, pointing to the oldest man in the room, "stand up!"

He did. He was the one who wasn't armed.

"You want to leave?"

"Oh, yessir," the old man said, nervously.

"Do you know who Gabriel Dye is?"

"Yessir."

"Is he here?"

"I-I don't think so, sir."

"When did you see him last?"

"E-early this mornin', when him and his gang left," he said.

"Okay," Clint said, "go."

"Sir?"

"Go! Get out!"

"Yessir."

The man ran to the doors and out of the saloon. Clint turned to the bartender.

"Dye was here this morning," he said. "He left with his gang. Do you know where they were going?"

"Well . . . I heard them say they were goin' to Goodwill."

"Right," Clint said, "and I was waiting for them there. The members of his gang are dead or in jail. He's the only one who got away, because he ran."

The bartender looked surprised.

"You two," Clint said to the other customers. "Come over here."

They both stood up and walked to the bar. One was in his forties, with a belly that hung over his belt, the other in his thirties, whipcord lean.

"Put your guns on the bar."

They both obeyed, and quickly.

"Put those under the bar," he told the bartender.

The man obeyed.

"I'm going to find Gabriel Dye and bring him back to Goodwill to pay for his crimes," Clint said. "Are either of you part of his gang?"

"No, sir," the fat one said.

"I just come here to drink," the thin one said.

"Have any of you seen him since this morning?"

The two men shook their heads, but the bartender just stood stiffly.

"There's a woman here who Dye visits," Clint said. "Who is she?"

"Well . . ." the bartender said.

"Spit it out!" Clint snapped. "I don't have all day."

"Um," the bartender said, "are you the law?"

"No," Clint said, "my name is Clint Adams."

"A-Adams?" the fat man said.

"The Gunsmith?" the skinny one asked.

"Why didn't you say so in the first place," the bartender said. "Dye's crazy. He scares the shit out of us whenever he comes here. If anybody can get rid of him, it's you."

"Have you seen him since this morning?" Clint asked, again.

"No," the bartender said, "but the woman you want is Ava. She's upstairs, second door."

"Is there a back way in and out of here?"

"Yeah," the bartender said.

Clint looked at the two customers.

"You two get out."

"What about our guns?" one asked.

"Come back later for them," Clint said. "And if I find out either of you warned Dye—"

"We wouldn't," the heavy one said.

"We're afraid of him, too," the thin one said. "If you can get rid of him—"

"Okay," Clint said, "get out."

As they left, he took his gun off the bar and put it in his holster.

"Second door?" he said.

"That's right."

"You stay here," Clint said. "I'm perfectly willing to kill Dye to take him back, and anybody who tries to stop me."

"I ain't gonna move from this spot," the bartender said.

"Good."

Clint turned and headed for the stairs.

Chapter Fifty-Three

Clint went up the stairs to the second door, put his right hand on his gun and knocked with his left. The woman who opened it was in her thirties, had a lush, full body that was on display due to a blue nightgown that was being held up—just barely—by thin straps. Her hair was long and blonde, her skin smooth and pale. She had been pretty once, but now her eyes seemed deep set and her mouth stern.

"I'm busy," she said, "come back tomorrow."

"Busy doing what?"

"What?" she said. "What do you think? My job."

"And what's that?" Clint asked. "What's your job?"

"I'm a whore," she said. "Have been for years."

"And is your name Ava?"

"That's right." She leaned against the door jamb, arms folded so that her breasts were lifted impressively.

"That's right," she said. "But like I said, I'm busy."

Clint reached out and pushed her door open all the way. There was no one in her bed, and the room—what he could see of it—was empty.

"You don't look busy," he said. "Are you expecting someone?"

She studied him and suddenly smiled—a smile that transformed her face.

"I changed my mind," she said. "Come on in, handsome."

She backed away from the door to let him enter. He closed the door behind him, looked around. There was no one else in the room, unless they were under the bed or in the closet.

"You mind?" he asked, pointing at the bed.

"Help yourself."

He leaned over to gaze under the bed, then walked across the room and pulled the closet door open. It was packed with dresses. He looked down but didn't push the dresses aside to look behind them.

When he turned to look at Ava, the nightgown was pooled around her feet. Her breasts were pear-shaped, with heavy undersides and large, pink nipples surrounded by wide aureole.

Clint's mouth went dry, but he wasn't there for sex.

"Do you know Gabriel Dye?"

"I do," she said. "He's a customer of mine."

"When's the last time you saw him?"

"About an hour ago," she said, and jerked her chin in the direction of the closet.

Clint waved her back toward the bed. She got on it, on her knees.

"Come on, handsome," she said, cradling her breasts in her hands. "Look what I got for ya."

Clint turned and faced the closet. He was going to get on the bed with the woman, grab a couple of hands full of her and wait for Dye to come out, but he changed his mind.

"Come on out, Dye," he said. "The dresses hid everything but your toes."

He stood there waiting patiently. Finally, the closet door slammed open and Gabriel Dye came running out, his gun in his hand, shouting something unintelligible.

Clint had wanted him alive, but the man wasn't giving him that choice. He drew quickly and fired. He could have shot him in the knee, or the arm, but that was trick shooting, and this wasn't the time for that. Dye made his way with his gun, and, if Clint did anything but his best, he would have been killed.

He shot Gabriel Dye in the chest. The bullet didn't stop his forward progression. Dye continued to stagger forward, and Ava had to leap off the bed to avoid him as he fell face down on the mattress.

She stood next to the bed, then, her hands on her hips, breasts thrust out and said, "He never looked better."

Chapter Fifty-Four

Clint found out from Ava that Dye was a longtime customer who she hated.

"He was brutal and liked to be told how good he was. So I told 'im, and he paid good. But I'm glad he's dead. He's crazy. This is about those holiday raids, right?"

"Yes."

"So you know he was crazy."

"Yes," Clint said, "I know."

Dye's blood was pooling beneath him, soaking her sheets.

"Now I gotta get new sheets," she complained. "Are you gonna get 'im out of here?"

"Yes, I am," Clint said. "I'll be taking him back to Goodwill. Is his horse in the back?"

"I think so."

"Okay, I'm going to need help. Go down and get the bartender, bring him up here."

"Right."

She started for the door.

"Maybe you better put something on, first."

She looked down at her nudity, said, "Oops," then picked up her nightgown, put it on and left the room.

***

The bartender and Clint wrapped the body in Ava's sheets and carried it down the back stairs. They found Dye's horse there and tied the body to the saddle. Then Clint went around to the front to collect the Tobiano.

"In the future," Clint told the bartender, "if anyone comes around to join his gang, tell them what happened."

"I will," the man said, "and thanks, Mr. Adams. We're glad to be rid of Gabriel Dye."

"You can give those fellas back their guns after I leave," Clint said.

"Oh, you won't get any trouble from them," the bartender said. "They just come here to sit and drink."

"Okay," Clint said, "thanks for your help. And here." He gave the bartender some money. "Tell Ava it's for her new sheets."

The bartender smiled and said, "She'll be real happy to get it, Mr. Adams. Thanks. I hope you get back to Goodwill in time to celebrate some of Christmas."

"Yes," Clint said. "I hope so, too."

***

It was dark when Clint got to Goodwill, but at least it was still Christmas. The celebration was going on in the street as he rode through, leading the horse with Gabriel Dye's body.

Torches had been lit so people could continue to celebrate in the dark. There were actually some musicians out, playing Christmas songs. Clint felt bad that two of the people he had used to defend the town were not seeing this activity. They were lying in the undertaker's office. He didn't know them well, didn't know if they had families.

As he approached City Hall, he saw the mayor standing out front, smiling and laughing. When he reached the politician, the music stopped, and it was as if everyone suddenly noticed him.

"You're back," Edgewater said, looking at the horse behind him. "Is that him?"

"That's him," Clint said. He dismounted, walked to the horse, and cut the ropes that were holding the body in place. The bloody sheet hit the ground and flapped open to reveal the body inside.

"Merry Christmas," Clint said to the mayor. "This was what you wanted."

The mayor walked to stand over the body, said, "You're damn right it is!"

He turned to the people who had crowded around.

"You should all know that this was the man who was going to destroy our town. But he's dead now, thanks to the Gunsmith. He and his gang will never attack another town on a holiday or any other day."

The people moved closer to take a look at the body. Some of them even spit on it—men and women both.

"He won't get a grave in our cemetery," the mayor said. "We'll bury him in a hole just outside of town. No marker. Because that's what he deserves. But for now, the body's going to stay right here for everyone to see." He turned toward the band. "Start the music again!"

They started playing, but Clint turned his back and mounted his horse.

"Aren't you going to stay to celebrate?" the mayor asked him.

"No," Clint said. "This is not my idea of a Christmas celebration. I've got somewhere else to go."

He turned the Tobiano and started riding through town, through the celebration. People tried to reach out to touch him, and thank him, but he neither slowed, nor did he acknowledge them. What was left of his Christmas was going to be spent with a mother and her little boy, if they would have him.

Chapter Fifty-Five

Clint made one stop on his way to Juliet's house, found what he wanted and put it in his pocket. Dexter was glad to give it up and replace it on his chest with a deputy's badge.

Clint reined in Toby in front of the house, dismounted and tied the horse off. Then he took a deep breath and knocked on the door. It was opened by Juliet, who stared at him for a moment, then hugged him.

"You're safe."

She drew him inside.

"And Dye?" she asked.

"Dead."

"Thank God."

"Joey?"

She nodded toward the tree. Clint saw the boy sitting in front of it, looking up at the flickering candlelight.

"Have you told him?" Clint asked.

"No. Like you said, I left it for you."

"Good."

He took his hat off and set it aside.

"Supper's almost ready," she said. "We waited."

"Thank you. It smells wonderful."

"It's a turkey," she said.

"I'll wash up," he said, "and then talk to the boy."

"I don't envy you," she said.

He washed his hands in the sink, then walked over to where Joey was sitting.

"Joey?"

"You're here," Jocy said, without looking at him.

"I told you I'd try to make it."

"That's what my Pa always said," Joey replied, "only he never did."

"He tried, Joey," Clint said, "he tried real hard."

Joey looked at him.

"How do you know?"

"Because I was with him," Clint said, "just before he was killed."

The boy's mouth fell open.

"My Pa's dead?"

"Yes," Clint said.

"But—"

"It happened even before I got here," Clint said. "If you want, I can tell you about it."

The boy hesitated, then said, "Yes, please."

Clint told Joey how Sheriff Owens had asked him to help him catch the three killers, so he could get back to Joey in time for Christmas.

"That was all we wanted to do, Joey," Clint said, "was get back to you before tonight."

"Why didn't you tell me before?" Joey asked.

"I was trying to figure out a way," Clint said, "but I wanted you to have Christmas Eve and Christmas Day before I told you."

"D-does my Ma know he's dead?"

"Yes," Clint said. "She found out a little while ago from the undertaker. That was why she kept you away from town, so nobody would tell you, until we were ready."

There were tears glistening in the boy's eyes like snowflakes.

"What happened to the men who killed him?" he asked.

"I killed them," Clint said.

"And did you get the bad man you were after today?" Joey asked.

"I did. It's all over. The town, and Christmas, are safe."

Juliet came up behind her son and put her hands on his shoulders.

"Ma—"

"I know, Joey," she said. "I'm sorry."

The boy wiped the tears from his eyes with the back of his hand.

"We're gonna have Christmas supper now, with Clint."

"And can we say a prayer for Pa?" he asked. "Can we?"

"We sure can. Why don't you get washed up."

Joey stood up and went to the kitchen to wash his hands.

"I have something for Joey," Clint said.

"You've bought him enough," Juliet said. "All the things you put under the tree for him."

"This is different."

He showed her what he was holding in his hand.

"Oh, yes," she said, and now there were tears in her eyes, not for her dead husband, but for her boy.

They walked to the kitchen table, where Joey had seated himself, waiting.

"Joey," she said, "Clint has something special for you."

"What is it?" Joey asked.

"It's something your father made me promise I'd give you, Joey," Clint said. He had stopped at the sheriff's office, hoping to find Dexter there, and when he did and told the man what he wanted, Dexter gave it up gladly.

Clint leaned down and pinned Sheriff Owens' badge onto Joey's shirt.

Joey's eyes went wide.

"Pa's badge!" he said, "look Ma, remember? Pa said he'd make me sheriff for the day."

"Yes, he did, Joey."

"And that's what you are today," Clint said. "You're Sheriff Joey."

Juliet looked at Clint, the tears now rolling down her cheeks, and said, "Merry Christmas. And now let's eat."

On Sale Now!

THE
GUNSMITH
GIANT
No. 2
The Life and Times of Clint Adams

Clint Adams has had enough of being the Gunsmith. Tired of drawing attention wherever he goes—tired of strangers who drew down on him just to make a name for themselves. When a Boston writer offers Clint the chance to write his life story, he thinks that this is a good way to set the record straight….

For more information
visit: www.SpeakingVolumes.us

On Sale Now!

THE
GUNSMITH
GIANT
No. 1
Trouble in Tombstone

**For more information
visit:** www.SpeakingVolumes.us

Coming December 27, 2020

THE GUNSMITH
465
The Children of Willow Springs

**For more information
visit:** www.SpeakingVolumes.us

On Sale Now!

THE GUNSMITH *series*
Books 430 – 464

**For more information
visit:** www.SpeakingVolumes.us

On Sale Now!

TALBOT ROPER NOVELS
by
ROBERT J. RANDISI

For more information
visit: www.SpeakingVolumes.us

On Sale Now!

Lady Gunsmith *series*
Books 1 - 9
Roxy Doyle and the Lady Executioner

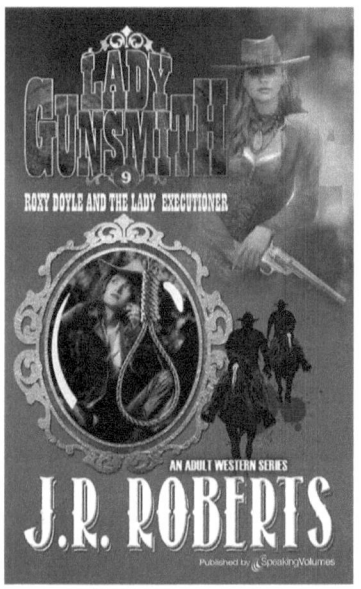

For more information
visit: www.SpeakingVolumes.us

On Sale Now!

Award-Winning Author
Robert J. Randisi (J.R. Roberts)

For more information
visit: www.SpeakingVolumes.us

Sign up for free and bargain books

Join the Speaking Volumes mailing list

Text
ILOVEBOOKS
to 22828 to get started.

Message and data rates may apply.

www.ingramcontent.com/pod-product-compliance
Lightning Source LLC
Chambersburg PA
CBHW050459260626
47157CB00004B/1118